MW01075329

Tales from Wasatch and Beyond

"Read and enjoy, but then take a look at the Epilogue. It's only then you truly appreciate the imagination that's gone into this neat blend of fact and fiction."

Zoë Sharp
Edgar, Barry, and CWA Dagger Award nominated author of the
Charlie Fox crime thriller series

"This, the fourth anthology, is the best of the series. Every story is tightly written and imaginative, giving the reader a lovely sense of the myths and legends of this section of the Utah Mountains. Some stories were creepy, some scary—but all fascinating. This is an excellent read. I recommend it highly."

Stan Trollip
Co-author of Barry Award winner for Best Paperback, Death of the Mantis

"At long last, fans of *Tales From H.E.L. and Beyond* and *Tales From Two-Bit Street and Beyond (Parts 1 and II)* can cuddle up with the latest local-flavored, spine-tingling story collection. But I have a complaint—I'll never be able to look at the featured landmarks and places the same again. If a cozy, happy story is what you're after, you've opened the wrong book—you'd better be good at turning pages with trembling hands!"

Wendy Toliver
Award-winning author of The Secret Life of a Teenage Siren,
Miss Match, and Lifted

"I was in awe with the talented writers in this book. Drienie and her merry band of authors did a great job. Each story was unique in its own way—spine-tingling and goose bumps, to say the least!"

Janet Battisti
Goodreads reviewer of 1,000+ books

"... a supernatural travel guide to Northern Utah—an expertly crafted, ingenious marriage of history and horror as told by some of northern Utah's most gifted writers. Serving up fictionalized accounts based on local hauntings and verifiable historical events, this collection acts as the ultimate ghostly anthology for anyone who's ever wondered what spirits lurk amid the towns of the Wasatch Mountain Range. Required reading for anyone with a taste for the supernatural who has ever lived in, traveled to, or plans to visit northern Utah."

Vince Font
Author of The Untold Story of the Falcon and the Snowman

"*Tales from the Wasatch and Beyond* is a wonderfully haunting mix of creepy and savage, melancholy and loss, death and redemption; all set in a background rich in history, folklore, and legend."

Marcia Lusk
Vice President, Utah Romance Writers of America 2004-2005

Tales from…
The Wasatch
and beyond…

Tales from the Wasatch Mountains…
Its People, Its Towns, and the Ghosts Who
Haunt Them

Drienie Hattingh

Compiled by: Drienie Hattingh
Published by Drienie Hattingh
Edited by: Precision Editing
Second Editing/Formatting by: Marley Gibson

Photography:
Cover: Johnny Adolphson
Inside: Johnny Adolphson, Drienie Hattingh, David Owen,
Ralph Maughan, Johan Hattingh, Jed Pearson, Kristan Cook Checketts, Vicki
Droogsma, Sherry Hogg, Dimitria Van Leeuwen and Wikipedia

Cover Design: Dimitria Van Leeuwen

Printed in the United States of America
Published by Cardinal Rules Press

1st Printing June 2014
2nd Printing October 2017

Cardinal Rules
——— PRESS ———

Tales from Beyond Series

Dedication

I dedicate this book to my beloved husband, Johan.
Thank you for your constant, loving support.
We scaled many a 'mountain' together—
it's all about the climb.
Ek is lief vir jou... verder as die verste ster...
The best is yet to be.

Table of Contents

Foreword

Drienie Hattingh

The name "Utah" comes from the Native American Ute tribe and means *people of the mountains*. And indeed, the stories in this book are about the mountains and its people and ghosts who now haunt them. Some of these towns are thriving and others are long-forgotten ghost towns. The tales are all based on real historic events and legends in these towns. You can read all about it in the epilogue.

The Wasatch mountain range is named after a Ute Indian name meaning "mountain pass" or "low place in a high mountain." It stretches approximately 160 miles, from Bear River (Utah/Idaho border) in the North to Mount Nebo, the highest peak at 11,877, near Nephi in central Utah. Other significant peaks from north to south include Willard Peak, Ben Lomond, Mount Ogden, Bountiful Peak, Mount Olympus, Lone Peak, Mount Timpanogos, Provo Peak and Loafer Mountain.

Since the earliest settlement, the majority of Utah's population has chosen to settle along the range's western front, known as The Wasatch Front.

These mountains were an important source of water, timber, and granite for early settlers. Today they continue to serve as the primary source of water and provide year-round recreational opportunities to residents and visitors alike.

The mountains were first viewed by white men in 1776. Fathers Francisco Atanasio Dominguez and Silvestre Velez de Escalante crossed the range, exiting near present-day Spanish Fork. In the 1820s fur traders from Santa Fe and Taos, such as Etienne Provost, for whom the city of Provo is named, arrived. Then came British and American trappers, including Peter Skene Ogden, for whom Ogden was named. The rivalry throughout the west, between British and American fur interests, stopped in 1840 when silk became fashionable.

The Native Americans—the Utes, Shoshoni and Blackfeet—who once called the Wasatch Mountains home, are long gone—but as you will learn from many of these stories, their spirits are still very much present.

In the 1860s silver, lead, and zinc deposits were discovered in the canyons and mountains southeast of Salt Lake City, including Big Cottonwood, Little Cottonwood, and Parley's Canyons. Ten years or so later towns like Alta and Park City had sprung up, developing as other mining towns in the West, including Ogden, where the Railroads met—overflowing with saloons, brothels and breweries. Their municipal revenues came mostly from saloon licenses and fines for prostitution. After years of decline, Alta and Park City turned into ski resorts and Ogden's downtown changed into a quaint area with antique stores, galleries, coffee shops and restaurants.

I now invite you to read the stories written by the authors who live in and around the Wasatch Mountains. They did their research and chose a town and legend, or historical event that spoke directly to them and wove their own stories around these documented incidents.

Drienie Hattingh

Introduction

Zoë Sharp

I have always loved collections of short stories where there's a definite theme in mind. And when it comes to writing short fiction, in some ways the more restrictions there are, the better it gets those creative juices flowing.

The most difficult stories, without doubt, are when an editor says, "Write about anything you like." I'd far rather have a common theme, a setting, even an obligatory type of character. On two occasions I've managed to incorporate the title of the anthology into the closing line. It all adds to the fun.

But when Drienie first approached me about writing this introduction, I didn't fully appreciate the ingenuity of the idea behind the anthology. Local Utah authors were set the task of researching a location in the Wasatch Mountains and uncovering a local myth or creepy tale that inspired them to come up with their own take.

Reading this collection has been a treat. The scale and imagination of the stories stretches from the Moby Dick of grizzly bears, campfire tales of giant wolves, a ghost train in the desert and the perils of staying just a little too long at the late-night antique store, via the lure of the stars—either above a midnight lake or spread across a movie theatre ceiling—making friends with new (and old) neighbors, and how far one brother will go for another, to the dangers of a disused silver mine, the restless souls of forgotten soldiers, a Native American legend, and a curse that follows a family for generations.

Read and enjoy, as I did, but then take a look at the Epilogue. It's only then you truly appreciate the imagination that's gone into this neat blend of fact and fiction. And it makes you want to go right back to the beginning and read through them all again, like being in on a very subtle joke.

But the theme running through all the tales—indeed, almost a character in its own right—has to be the wild and beautiful Wasatch Mountains and the people of those mountains.

It's been an honor to be involved, however briefly.

Zoë Sharp

Zoë Sharp opted out of mainstream education at age twelve and wrote her first novel when she was fifteen. She created the no-nonsense heroine of her highly acclaimed Charlotte "Charlie" Fox crime thriller series after receiving death-threat letters as a photojournalist. Zoë's work has been used in school textbooks in Denmark, made into a short film, optioned by Twentieth Century Fox TV, and nominated for numerous awards including the Edgar, Anthony, Barry, Benjamin Franklin, and Macavity in the United States, as well as the CWA Dagger Award in the UK. Zoë lives in the English Lake District. Her hobbies are sailing, fast cars, motorbikes, target shooting, travel, films, music, and reading. **http://www.ZoeSharp.com**

Mount Logan, *at 9,710 feet, is the highest point south of the Logan Canyon in the Bear River Range. It is the 39th highest mountain in Utah.*

I. Nemesis

Drienie Hattingh

He's here, I can smell him. This time he will not get away. I will hunt him down and get my revenge for all he and his brothers have done to me and mine.

Jeremiah spat the tobacco juice through the air, leaving a brown trail across the pure white snow. He ached to his bones after tracking a moose all day long. Despite his layers of clothing, he was wet and cold and his hands pulsed with the cold and his face was so numb he could hardly move his jaw. Although the snow helped him with tracking, he was discouraged and irritable and decided to call it a day.

He had wanted to get the moose and catch a bear cub he'd seen with its mother earlier. This wouldn't be the first time Jeremiah took a cub from its mother. Bear cubs were good money. He smiled and thought, *as easy as taking candy from a kid.* All he had to do was wait around after the mother bear put her cub up in a tree. She did this by walking the cub to a big tree where she would growl and snap at it to send it scurrying up into branches. She would then leave and go hunting for food.

While she was away, Jeremiah would quickly climb up the tree, grab the cub before it sent distress calls to its mother, and stuff it into a bag. Jeremiah stifled his laughter as he imagined the mother bear frantically searching for her cub in the tree where she'd left him... and the next tree, and the next tree, as though she'd made a mistake, not remembering where she'd left him. He would have loved to hang around and watch the mother's reaction but knew she would probably kill him if she smelled his presence.

Jeremiah was about to set up camp when he looked across the ravine and saw a movement in the foothills on the opposite mountain. He crouched down slowly and then carefully parted the pine branches in front of him with a rough, callused hand while he lifted the binoculars to his eyes.

Someone else looking through the binoculars would probably see only the tree-covered mountain and the blue sky, but Jeremiah saw something else. His mouth formed into a soundless whistle as he took in the scene. Using both hands now, he turned the lens to enlarge the gray speck that moved across an open green meadow between the evergreens on the mountain slope.

"It's him," he whispered, "It's the biggest grizzly I've seen in the mountains since ol' three-toes."

As Jeremiah looked at the bear, he recalled the first time he saw this monstrous animal—two years ago, in the hunting season.

He had been on his own as usual, ready to make camp and a fire to warm up some beans. But something attracted his attention. The sun was still bright enough when he reached for his binoculars.

At first he hadn't been able to make out exactly what it was. Then he thought it could be a big bull moose—he would love to take home a real nice rack. He had always felt a bit sheepish when his other hunter friends came over for beer and pizza and saw the small rack he had on the wall in his den. They all had enormous racks on their walls, compared to the one he had.

He had moved as fast and as quietly as he could, down the hill and through the small canyon to the other side where he last saw the animal. There was enough light left for him to get a good shot at the moose. He was glad for the slight breeze in his direction... the animal wouldn't be able to smell him.

He could still remember the shock that travelled through his body at the scene; his head jerked back sharply. It wasn't a giant moose he saw over the outcropping of rocks—it was the biggest grizzly he had ever seen. He marveled at the magnificent animal. How many times did he tell those know-it-all hunters that ol' Ephraim wasn't the last grizzly in the Wasatch Mountains? He had seen tracks in the forests ever since he started hunting in his teens— tracks that could only belong to a grizzly. And here he had proof, right there in front of him—at least 1,000 lbs. worth of proof.

He had crouched down again and quietly loaded the rifle. But then, when he carefully rose and peeked over the rocks, ready to take aim, the bear was gone. That was the last time he had seen the big grizzly.

Later when he and his friends met for breakfast at Cracker Barrel in Paradise, they wouldn't believe him. They said it couldn't have been a grizzly; it must have been a brown bear. But he knew it was a grizzly. Not only did it have the distinctive hump over the front shoulders, but it had that coloring of the hair—the "silver tips."

But that was *then*. Now he was here again and *this* time he would get the beast. His hands clenched and his eyes narrowed. He would do whatever it took to get this magnificent trophy. His friends would eat their words when he invited them over to his place for a couple of beers and he'd smile as they looked at the massive head on his den wall and the huge silver-tip hide on his floor.

Jeremiah looked through the binoculars and saw the bear lift his enormous head and move as if to sniff the air. The beast reared up on his hind legs and seemed to look straight at him. "Shit!" Jeremiah muttered under his breath and then laughed a bit hesitantly telling himself the bear could not see him at such a distance.

Mesmerized, he looked on as the creature dropped back on all fours and started moving down the mountain in his general direction. *At least I don't have to track him,* Jeremiah thought as he quickly opened his backpack. He took out a plastic bag with a piece of steak he wanted to cook for dinner. Instead he'd use it as bait, to lure the beast to him.

He pulled a branch of an aspen down and, with his knife, trimmed it into a sharp point to spear the meat. Next he cleared leaves from the ground below the hanging meat and rummaged through his backpack again to pull out the metal trap. He opened the sharp jaws, set it, and laid it on the cleared spot under the bait. Finally, he camouflaged it with leaves.

Back in 1923 another hunter had done exactly the same thing, and in so doing had caught the biggest grizzly in recorded history. That was the bear that became known as Ol' Ephraim. That grizzly didn't stand a chance. After he stepped into the jaws of the trap and it closed around his three-toed foot, the hunter took aim and didn't stop shooting until the rifle was emptied into the howling beast's enormous skull.

History will repeat itself tonight, thought Jeremiah. He gathered his backpack and other belongings and hid them under bushes. He didn't have a lot of time and he knew it. *The grizzly will be here soon.* He took position behind a big pine tree.

His rifle was loaded and pressed against his shoulder—ready to fire.

Jeremiah waited for some time, longer than he thought it would take the grizzly to come. Then he heard a sound, but the sound didn't come from in front of him like he had expected. It came from behind. He slowly turned around, the hair on his neck stood on end.

Right behind him, just a few feet away, stood the grizzly, stretched to his full height on his hind legs—about ten feet tall. Stunned, Jeremiah stood there. It was as though he stared into the eyes of Lucifer himself. When he recovered from the shock, he fired straight at the beast's head, aiming for the spot between his eyes.

Jeremiah looked on in disbelief. The bullet hit its target full force, but there was no blood and the beast didn't seem to feel anything. It just opened its jaws wide and let out a long terrifying roar, as if to remind the hunter of all the wrong he and his kind had done.

The beast's growls and foul breath washed over the hunter as his final gaze fixed on the grizzly's left foot. It had three toes.

At last, the revenge is mine.

Crawford Mountains, *at 8,000 feet, towers over the flat grass-covered Bear River Valley terrain. Randolph lies in this valley at 6,280 feet at the feet of these mountains. The Bear River winds through the valley to the east of the town. In the distance, to the south, loom the Uinta Mountains with its 14,000 foot peaks. To the west lies the Wasatch Mountain Range with the Wyoming border a stone throw away. 483 people calls Randolph home. It is still a ranching community.*

2. Night of the Wolves

Michele McKinnon

Jack and Cody plodded up the gravel lane on the back of Jack's trusty old horse, Sadie. They were on their way to a great adventure—they were going on a camping trip—alone. Although Jack and his best friend, Cody, lived with their families in the small northern Utah town of Randolph, they had spent many happy hours on Jack's family ranch located about three miles southwest of the town.

Jack's grandpa told them the ranch and the surrounding area used to be a town called Argyle, but now there were only a few derelict houses and buildings scattered around. Jack's dad grew mostly alfalfa to feed the cows and sheep during the harsh valley winters. Grandpa said that during some

17

winters he had seen the temperatures drop to fifty below zero.

But it was summer now, and Jack and Cody were ready for some fun.

Ha, Jack thought, *we're men now—thirteen and alone in the wilderness. We can handle anything nature has to throw at us. We'll be like Grandpa and his brothers—out roaming the hills. Sadie will be our wild mustang and we'll have to break her and train her to round up the cows.* Jack laughed out loud as he looked down at the fat old buckskin horse beneath them, slowly making her way up the gravel road.

"What are you laughing at?" Cody asked. "We're not having fun yet and Sadie's as slow as molasses in January."

"You could always walk," Jack teased. "Actually I was trying to pretend she was one of those wild mustangs the Indians used to catch and break, but when I looked down at her I had to laugh. Poor old Sadie—at least she's reliable and won't dump us off in a ditch somewhere."

The sun tilted toward the west when the boys finally got to the ranch.

"I'll get the gate," Cody said as he slid off the side of the fat old mare.

"Just leave the gate open; there aren't any cows or sheep here right now," Jack said.

"Sure," Cody said. "And don't let that wild mustang you're riding get spooked and run away with you." He laughed as he opened the gate and let

Jack and Sadie through and followed them the short distance down to the barn.

The weathered old barn was still solid and had a large corral on one side. The boys led Sadie into the corral and unloaded their pack, bedrolls, and trusty .22 rifles. Then they took off her saddle and bridle, and pumped water from the hand pump on the old well into a bucket and fed her some of the fragrant alfalfa stored in the barn.

"It's so great to be up here alone," Jack said as he rolled out his sleeping bag inside the little pup tent they had packed in. "I can't believe it was so hard getting our parents to let us come. You'd think we were little kids or something."

"Yeah, well I guess we aren't alone. Look there."

Jack looked in the direction Cody pointed. The setting sun glinted off Grandpa's old red truck coming up the long dirt lane, leaving a cloud of dust behind it. Jack smiled. It would be fun to have Grandpa here even if they were supposed to be camping alone.

"Hi boys," Grandpa said stepping out of the truck after he pulled up next to their tent. "Ah ... your mothers sort of *influenced* me to come out and check on you two. I told them that you were young men now and didn't need a nursemaid, but they insisted, so I brought along a chair, some homemade root beer, and marshmallows. We might as well enjoy some time around the campfire."

Jack didn't say so out loud, but he was glad Grandpa was there. He looked forward to the tales

Grandpa would inevitably spin for them. His stories always kept Jack and his friends riveted. Jack could picture the ranch as it was back in the old days when Grandpa was a boy growing up here in Argyle, with his sixteen brothers and sisters. The two-story ranch house and all of the hustle and bustle seemed to spring to life again.

Their favorite stories were about when Grandpa was young and the many times he and his brothers got into trouble. If it was summer, rather than face a switching from their father, they would grab a bedroll and some food and head for the hills. Sometimes they stayed away for several days at a time, or at least until they figured Great Grandpa had cooled off or forgot their offences. Life on the ranch was so busy Great Grandpa probably did forget, especially with seventeen children.

After a shared dinner of beans, hot dogs, and the treats Grandpa brought, he leaned back in his chair, picked a long piece of grass to chew on, and breathed a contented sigh.

"Grandpa, please tell us some of your stories," Jack begged.

"Yeah, those stories about how it used to be, back in the old days, when you were a boy," Cody added.

Grandpa grinned as he leaned forward in his chair, the fire lighting his face up. "Well now, back in the olden days, the Shoshone and Bannock Indians sometimes passed through this area in the summer. They would camp along the creek, just on the north edge of our property. They usually stayed a couple of weeks, fishing, hunting, and breaking some of the wild horses they had rounded up. My dad, your great-grandfather, was friendly with these Indians, and when he found that they had raided his garden, Dad just had us boys plant extra the next year. And sometimes Mother gave them fresh baked bread.

"But there was this one day when my little brother and I were left alone on the ranch for a short while. I think I was only eight and my brother was six. We were playing around the corrals and outbuildings when we looked up and saw some Indians riding down through those sagebrush hills on horseback."

Grandpa pointed south to the hills just above the ranch. "We had never been afraid of these peaceful people before, but being alone, our imagination ran away with us and we panicked. We both ran to the barn as though our lives depended on it. Once inside, we crawled under the hay in the manger and pulled it on top of us. We didn't even dare breathe. We heard the horses outside the barn and the Indians dismounting. I peeked out through the hay. There stood five very large Indian men. They were pointing to where we were hiding and laughing at us. They finally saluted a goodbye to our still hidden forms and rode off."

"That is so funny, Grandpa." Jack said laughing. "I guess it would be scary out here with you and Great Uncle Andy all alone. It's a good thing those guys were friendly or you and your little brother would have been toast."

"Yeah," Cody said poking his finger into Jack's chest, "and you would never have been born, Wise Guy. Tell us another story, please, Grandpa."

"All right, let me think. This is one I don't believe I've told you before. It happened much later in my life. We were living on the ranch then too, but I was married to your grandmother by then. We had two children—Jack, your father, was our oldest, but he was too little to remember this—he was only about three or four when the *wolves* came." Grandpa reached out and put some more wood on the campfire. "It had been a bitter cold winter that year, and we began seeing huge wolves in the valley that had migrated down from Canada. These wolves could take down a full-grown steer and eat it all in one night, leaving nothing but the hooves, horns, and some bones."

"It was also one of those huge wolves that got my brother's beautiful Belgian stallion. It was a large horse and must have put up a valiant fight. The brush was torn up and blood was spattered all over the snow—there wasn't much left of the poor horse. My uncle finally killed one of the biggest wolves. He had it made into a rug with the head still attached. I've never seen a coyote, dog, or another wolf that big."

Jack and Cody shivered even though it was a warm summer night. "Grandpa, did they ever get all the wolves to leave the valley?"

"Well now, Jack, I don't rightly know. What I do know is that they tried trapping and hunting the wolves, but they were wily devils. It took some mighty crafty trappers to get a wolf back then. They said that one of those wolves could actually rip the trap jaws right out of the frame. The ranchers must have at least discouraged them a little because the killings finally stopped."

Grandpa paused and looked over his shoulder, then leaned toward the boys and said in a loud whisper. "But some folks say they can still hear them howling on a quiet night."

The boys both looked over their own shoulders and edged closer to the fire.

Grandpa stood up and stretched his legs. "Well lads, I've got to be going. Your grandmother will wonder what happened to me. Besides, I'm way too old to sleep on the ground, and I know you boys don't want me hanging around. You be careful now and don't let any of them wolves get you." Grandpa grinned as he walked toward his old pickup truck. "I'll come back and check on you in the morning."

The boys watched as he climbed into the cab of the truck, started the engine, and drove off waving goodbye.

With his eyes on the departing truck, Cody said, "Jack, do you think your grandpa was trying to scare us?"

"I don't know Cody, but I'm sure we don't have anything to worry about. Like he said, the killings stopped a long time ago," Jack said trying to sound brave. "Come on, let's check on Sadie one more time and then try to get some sleep."

The boys slept fitfully as the full moon slowly rose above their little camp. Suddenly Jack woke with a start and sat straight up, listening intently. He shook Cody awake. "Listen," he said "I thought I heard Sadie." He lifted the tent flap and peered out. The moon revealed peaceful fields spreading away to the north. There was a growing mist moving up from the creek. It seemed to take on the shape of horses. Jack rubbed his eyes and the mist disappeared. The boys listened intently, but there was utter silence—then they heard the wild, terrified screams of a horse, accompanied by growling and snarling.

"Cody, come on! Sadie's in trouble." The boys pulled on their boots, grabbed their guns, and scrambled out of the tent. The screams and growls were coming from the far end of the corral.

The boys leapt over the corral fence and started running toward the terrible sounds. Then they stopped short. The hair on the back of Jack's neck stood up. The moonlit scene before them was a nightmare. The body of a horse lay in a pool of blood surrounded by a pack of huge wolves all growling and tearing at it. As the boys watched in horror, the biggest wolf turned his gaze on the boys and growled. His yellow eyes gleamed and his muzzle dripped with fresh red blood. Slowly the whole pack turned toward them. "Run Cody!" Jack yelled as the wolves leapt at them.

The boys sprinted into the barn and slammed the heavy wooden door. They pulled the big two-by-four down into the braces just as something hit the outside of the door with a force that made it shudder. There was a scraping noise like giant claws ripping the boards, and whining and growling and then momentary silence. Again, a great weight hit the door, followed by more scratching and growling.

"Come on, Jack," Cody said. "We can't let them get in. They'll tear us apart sure as they did poor old Sadie. Maybe we can shoot at them through the window up there and at least scare them away."

They scrambled up a stack of baled hay against the front wall of the barn and looked out the window. A snarling mass of fur leaped at them from below. Monster-sized wolves pawed and scratched at the door, leaving deep grooves down the old wood. They seemed to take turns hurling their heavy bodies against the door.

Both boys steadied their shaking arms against the high windowsill, taking careful aim. They had plenty of ammunition back in the tent, but here they only had what was in their guns and a few odd shells in their pockets. They fired directly at the head of the biggest animal. Nothing happened. The wolves continued their relentless attack. The boys fired again and again, certain they were hitting their target. A white mist rolled up from the creek and covered the wolves.

Stunned, the boys looked down at the quiet scene below. The only evidence that the wolves had been there were the deep grooves scratched into the barn door. Then they heard whinnying, and the sound of horse's hooves running.

"Cody," Jack said, "Look down by the creek."

In the distance, racing toward the barn were five beautiful pale horses, manes and tails streaming back as they ran. Atop each horse sat a young Indian brave. They rode low, leaning forward until their long, black hair mingled with the manes of their horses. They moved with their mounts so effortlessly that they seemed to become one with the magnificent animals.

They reined in just under the window. One of the Indians pointed up at the boys and said, "You ride with us tonight. The giant wolves will return and they will prowl and hunt until dawn. You must leave or become their prey."

The boys looked at each other but then they heard a howl in the distance. Jack grabbed Cody's arm. "Come on; we can't stay here, the wolves are back." He quickly helped Cody down onto the horse behind the first Indian, and then jumped on behind the next Indian. The horses bolted forward just as the wolves came around the corner of the barn snapping and snarling. The lead wolf made a mighty lunge and grabbed Jack's leg with his teeth. Jack screamed, but the speed of the horse pulled Jack and his leg out of the wolf's jaws. Jack knew the wolf had bitten him but, strangely, he didn't feel anything.

They rode up into the hills, leaving a trail of dust behind them. Jack held onto the Indian in front of him for all he was worth and hoped Cody was doing the same. It was impossible to ask questions. The rough ground seemed to fly beneath the horse's feet. Every time Jack turned around, he could see the wolves' sharp teeth gleaming white and red in the moonlight. He could almost feel their hot breath on the back of his neck. It seemed like they rode for hours, and Jack couldn't tell where they were going—maybe they were riding in circles.

His legs and arms ached. He didn't know how much longer he could hang on. Just then he saw a very faint glow in the sky over the Crawford Mountains in the East. The Indians slowed their horses. The growling ceased and the wolves seemed to disappear. Jack looked around and realized they were back at the ranch, next to their tent.

"Shouldn't we keep going?" Cody asked. "The wolves are going to come back."

"It will be dawn soon, and the wolves have left us," the Indian in front of Cody said.

"Thank you for saving our lives," Jack said. "I don't know what we would've done if you hadn't helped us."

"Your great-grandfather was a good friend. My people do not forget a friend," the Indian in front of Jack said. "This is the night your uncle killed the wolf leader, and the wolves do not forget either. They return every year on this night searching for your uncle or his people, seeking revenge."

Jack gulped as he and Cody slid off the horses. "Do you mean they were ghost wolves?"

But as soon as their feet touched the ground the Indians' horses were running. The boys could only stand and watch as they rode off.

"Can you believe that?" Cody said in a shaky voice. "We would have been wolf food without those guys. They saved our skin."

"I don't know where they came from, but I'm mighty glad they did," Jack said trying to steady his shaking legs.

"Yeah," Cody said. "I didn't think Indians rode around here anymore."

"I don't know what to think," Jack said, unsure whether the Indians had disappeared in the morning mist or into the hills.

Jack shivered, and then shook it off. "Come on, let's see if there is anything we can do for Sadie."

"What about your leg? I saw one of the wolves grab you."

"Oh, I forgot about it," Jack said, examining his leg. "There isn't even a tear in my pants. Not a scratch. How weird is that? Maybe ghost wolves can't really hurt you. Come on, maybe Sadie is okay too if those wolves really were ghosts."

The boys ran to the corral and vaulted over the rails. There were no traces of the grizzly scene they had witnessed the night before. But Sadie was gone too—not a sign of her, only her saddle and bridle hanging over the fence.

Tears trickled down Jack's face. Sadie was such a good old horse. When he was barely old enough to walk, he had learned to ride on her sturdy, safe back. He could hear Cody sniffling too. They quickly gathered up their things just as the first ray of sun peeked over the Crawford Mountains.

"Ya, you know Jack, I just can't believe they were all ghosts."

"Neither can I," Jack said. "Those horses and Indians felt pretty solid. Maybe Grandpa can help us figure it all out when he comes—boy have we got a story to tell him."

As they closed the gate, Jack looked down the lane and there was Sadie about a half a mile off running toward home as if her life depended on it. And further down, he saw the bright red of Grandpa's truck.

"Look Cody, it's Sadie! She's alive! I can't see any blood on her at all. Maybe the dead horse was a ghost horse too.

But as Cody turned around to look at the barn one last time, he grabbed Jack's arm, pointing with a shaking finger at the barn doors. Deep fresh grooves were clearly visible, and the smiles on their faces slid into looks of horror, as they heard the eerie howling of a wolf pack off in the distance.

The boys bolted, running as if Satan's own hounds were upon them, and who knows—maybe they were.

Wellsville Mountains, *with its highest peak, Boxelder, at 9,372 feet are located in the northern end of the Wasatch Range—between Brigham City and Cache Valley. The Range is **basically** one high, steep ridge the entire length. They are extremely rugged and are considered to be the steepest mountain range in the United States.*

3. Standing Guard

Vicki Droogsma

Jenna hurried to her car. She had stayed way too late at *Furniture and More*, the quaint antique store in the hills of Brigham City. The store was one of her favorite places, full of old furniture and hidden treasures.

She had wandered the building thinking about the soldiers who had convalesced here when this building was an operational military hospital. Her grandmother had volunteered then, and had told her stories about the soldiers.

Jenna stopped to look out the window at the paintings of circus animals lining some of the walls outside of the hallway connecting the furniture store with the antique store. She had asked one of the employees about them—were they leftover art from the days when this location was an Indian School?

The woman had told her no—they were painted when the building was used as a daycare about twenty years ago.

She walked quickly to her car as the sun sank slowly over the city, but stopped to watch the sunset. Orange streaks crossed the pale blue sky. When she turned back to her car she was startled to find a young woman standing right behind her. She was thin and pale with dark greasy hair hanging over her eyes.

"Please, please help me!" the woman said frantically, wringing her hands, holding a leash. "My dog, Jack, has gone into one of the buildings and won't come out."

Jenna hesitated, but the woman looked so sad and anxious, she couldn't say no and followed her around to another building. There was a door partially open, and they stepped inside. Jenna could faintly hear the sound of a dog whining somewhere within. The woman led her down steps into one of the tunnels beneath the structure. It had been built when the site was a military hospital during World War II. The dog's whimpering grew louder as they moved deeper into the darkness.

Footsteps suddenly sounded behind Jenna and then a rough bag came down over her head. She struggled, her nails digging at the arm that was encircling her throat, but it was no use. She couldn't breathe. Her heart raced painfully in her chest. She was caught, dragged for a short distance, and then dumped into what felt like a box. The bag was removed and Jenna found she was in a dog cage; the kind meant for large breeds.

The musty room made her nose itch. She could see dark stains on the walls and smelled the copper tang of blood. The blood splotches marred the graffiti on the wall. Debris lay scattered on the floor—broken chairs, paint cans. A pot filled with something vile-smelling stood against a wall. A limp form lay in one corner, its fur glistening wet.

Jenna shivered in fear as the smell of blood lingered. She heard voices in the middle of the room but could not make out what they said.

Something dripped on her neck. She looked up in the dim light; a furry form hung above her. A large drop of blood oozed down and hit her on the face. She screamed and pushed herself as far away as the cage allowed her to. Straining her neck, she peered out.

There were three of them—all wearing jeans and dark shirts. One wore a long, black cloak. He stood before a table upon which he had set several dark candles. He reached into a bag and pulled out a sharp, strangely curved knife.

She huddled in the cage, shaking. Who were these people? What were they going to do with her? She looked at the dead animal in the corner; then at the man standing at the table arranged with candles, and the knife. Then she knew. *Sacrifice!*

The one in the cloak started to speak. He chanted foreign words as he lit the candles, then he nodded to one of the others.

"Lord Satan." He intoned as one of the others opened the cage and grabbed her roughly by her arm. He yanked as she scrambled to hold on to the sides, nearly ripping out her nails as she did. She fought him as best she could, but he was stronger.

The one at the box continued speaking while she was pulled toward him. She thrashed and bit and screamed, the noise drowning out the words of the caped man. They held her down as she struggled.

The cloaked man lifted the knife and spoke some more. She did not hear the words over her own screams. Her vision filled with the gleaming blade as he held it over her. Her flesh tingled as she felt something evil forming around them. The room appeared darker despite the warm glow from the candles. It grew chilly. The iciness of the air sank into her skin and made her blood turn cold. She smelled the stench of death and decay in the smoke of the burning candles.

Something reached for her from the darkness, something demonic and evil. She could feel its talons reaching, grabbing for her soul. She struggled harder—nearly tearing her joints from their sockets. The cloaked one smiled and lifted the knife higher. She watched the knife begin its descent, glinting in the candlelight. The darkness smothered her, seeping into her core. It grasped at her spirit; she could feel it seize her soul. Despair filled her mind.

"You're going to die here." The darkness seemed to whisper. She believed it.

The knife inched closer, creeping with the agonizing slowness of a nightmare. The point touched her blouse between her belly button and her ribs, and then passed beyond. She felt the metal pierce her skin, felt blood trickle down her stomach.

Then she saw him. A tall man stood in the doorway of the dank room. A man dressed in some sort of soldier's uniform. His head was wrapped in a bandage that crossed his forehead. She stared in amazement when she realized she could see the hallway through him.

The darkness ebbed, backing away when the soldier entered the room. His mouth moved but she could hear nothing but her own screams.

The others had also seen him, their eyes widening as they saw the soldier pass through the debris on the floor. The dagger withdrew and Jenna clutched her bleeding stomach. She pulled out of the grasp of the ones holding her down.

Wildly, still clutching her stomach, she ran out the door into the hallway. There she saw more soldiers. They marched toward the little room of death. She slipped past them not daring to touch their ethereal bodies and burst out of the broken door into the cool night air.

She turned to the antique store, not wanting to, but drawn to have one more look at the horror she left behind. Through the windows, she could see many soldiers standing at attention, standing guard. Faint screams from the building reached her.

And then the cloaked man emerged—his cape tattered and bloody. He reached out to clutch her arm but incorporeal hands grabbed him. He screamed as he was dragged back into the shadows.

And then there was silence, except for her own gasping breaths.

The soldiers faded then, but she could still feel their presence. Still feel their eyes watching, waiting.

She ran to her car, struggling to find the keys she had put in her pocket. She climbed in and raced to the hospital, hoping she would make it before she bled to death. Should she go to the police? And tell them what?

That Satanists had kidnapped her for a sacrifice, and she had been saved by ghost soldiers?

Maybe not. Maybe a back street mugging would be more believable.

Whatever the case, she would never return to her favorite antique store; never go back to Brigham City.

DOVE CREEK, PROMONTORY POINT

The Golden Spike National Historic site is located about 38 miles west of Brigham City on Highway 83, near Promontory Point. 'Dove Creek Sinks' are located near Kelton. It can be reached by an old railroad grade. It's not recommended to venture out alone into the desert.

4. Flyin'

Christy Monson

Summer of 1880

Matthew's rumpled brown hair fell into his eyes. He brushed it away. "I hate my limp. I hate my stiff leg. I hate my life. I hate myself." He smashed his fist against his knee, sending shots of pain up and down his body.

"You're in a great mood today," said his friend Josh. "Thanks for the cheer-up."

Matthew scowled. "Don't walk with me, then."

"Oh, you know I'm always up for a dose of sour lemons. It's my favorite drink."

Matthew spat. A train whistle sounded far away.

"I want to fly. Be rid of that accident. It's going to haunt me all my life."

"You're just lucky your mother begged the doctor not to cut it off."

Matthew looked off into the distance. "I listen to those trains coming through here, and I want to drive one—fly down the tracks—away from all of this."

"You know you can never do that," said Josh. "You could never get hired as an engineer. Not with your leg."

"Thanks for stating the obvious."

Matthew bent down and pounded his fist on his knee again. The pain felt good.

"At the risk of offending your sourness. . ." Josh made a deep bow. "... I'd like to change the subject. Did you hear the story Jed Davis told his retired railroad buddies when he got back from Dove Creek yesterday?"

"No." Matthew turned to look at him. "How could I? You know I've been helping Pa in the milking shed all day."

"Well," Josh cleared his throat. "Davis went up the grade near the old Dove Creek Camp, and he heard the distant sound of a locomotive."

Matthew took a deep breath and chuckled. "Maybe Davis has something wrong with his ears."

Hearing the sound of a locomotive is no big deal. Someone could imagine they heard a train. He sighed.

"But trains don't run out there anymore." He scratched his head. "What was he doin' out there anyway?"

"Camping out overnight, I guess," said Josh. "He heard the whistle about midnight and left his tent to see what it was. When he got out by the tracks, he could see a light in the distance."

"It's all a stupid made-up story." Just then the sound of a train whistle whined in Matthew's head. "Did you just hear a train?"

"No," said Josh. "You know the train's not due for another hour."

It must be my imagination, thought Matthew. *I'm going coo coo*. He listened again, but the sound was gone. He shivered—couldn't let on what just happened. So he turned to go.

"Wait." Josh clutched his arm. "There's more. After Davis saw a light in the distance, he went back to his tent to get his old rifle."

"Smart man to take a gun with him. Who knows what's up there."

"On his way back to the tent he heard voices *and,* get this, they were speaking Chinese."

Matthew stopped walking and turned to stare at Josh. "Dove Creek was a camp for the Chinks that worked the railroad, but give me a break."

"I know, I know, it sounds crazy," said Josh, "but that's what Davis saw."

Matthew snorted at him. "He didn't *see* it, he *heard* it."

"Oh, yeah, sorry," said Josh.

"I gotta go," said Matthew. "Pa needs me to pitch some hay down from the top of the barn."

"Beats me how you climb those ladders with that bum leg."

Matthew could feel tension creep up his body. "I hate my leg!"

"I'll see you later." Josh waved and walked toward town.

Matthew limped up the lane. *Maybe I'll check out Dove Creek*, he thought. *I'd love to fly down the tracks even if it's with those Chinks.* Whispers of Chinese gibberish seemed to wrap themselves around him. He turned around to see where the sound came from. But it was in his head, and he knew it. He shook himself.

What's wrong with me? I'm going crazy.

Matthew dragged himself into the barn and climbed the ladder, mumbling. "Why is it always me that has to get the hay, and me that has to do the milking, and me that has to muck out the stalls?"

"Because you're all I have to help me," said Pa.

Matthew jumped. "What are you doin' up here, Pa?"

"Just repairing the barn roof over in the west corner where it leaked."

"Sorry you heard me complainin.'"

"Look, son, I know it's tough. It's too bad about your leg. I wish things were different, but with your mother ailin' and unable to help, I got no one else."

"I know, Pa." Josh squeezed the pitch fork handle and released it. He felt guilty that Pa heard him. Pa was getting old and needed him.

"I wish Cassie were still alive," said Pa.

"She wouldn't help with the farming," said Josh.

"No, but she would cheer your mother up some and give a hand with the house work."

Matthew missed his older sister but not her advice. Even after he was grown, she would still tell him what to do—up until she got sick. Cholera had hit only two families in Kelton. *Why did one of them have to be ours?* thought Matthew.

Matthew finished his chores and hobbled toward Josh's lane.

Josh walked up the road. "Hey. What's up?"

"I've been thinkin' about heading out to Dove Creek." Matthew rubbed his hands together. Chinese voices began to dispute in his head again, just like before when he thought about going out to Dove Creek. Fear weighted his stomach down like a pile of rocks.

A distant train whistle echoed behind the foreign talk. He quit walking and shook himself. "Stop!" he yelled at the noise in his head. *What's the matter with me?* he wondered. Maybe if he went out there, he could talk the Chinks into getting' out of his head, but he couldn't tell Josh that. "I want to find me some ghost train and ride it."

"I ... I," stammered Josh. "You might never come back. Besides, I don't know that I really believe Davis. He's an old geezer just talkin' through his hat."

"Maybe he is, and maybe he isn't," said Matthew. "That's what I aim to find out." The Chinese arguing got louder in his head.

"How are you going to get out there?"

"Walk."

"You can't walk with your leg. It's just too far."

"Yes, I can."

"What'll you tell your folks?"

"I already told them that I'm at your house."

"Wait! You going right now?"

"Yep." Matthew hobbled toward the sagebrush at the edge of town.

"At least follow the road," said Josh.

"Shortest way is best." Matthew spoke to the air as he headed out across the desert. Train whistles and arguing whined in his ears. *Stop it!* he thought. *Just quit!*

Josh hurried to catch up.

They walked for an hour. With each step, pain-like needles shot down Matthew's leg and up into his torso.

The mournful whistle in his head got louder.

Two hours. With each cry of the train whistle, agonizing pain seemed to burn through his entire body.

Matthew crumpled into the sand. "Can't do it. Pain's too bad." He rubbed his leg.

"Let's go back and get a wagon."

"Can't," said Matthew. "Pa needs it."

"We can take our wagon."

Matthew looked at him in disgust. "If we take your wagon, your folks will tell Pa. I don't want anyone to know."

"I'll get one of our horses, and we'll take that old buckboard that's out behind the hotel."

Matthew rubbed his hands together. "That'll work." He limped to his feet, and they headed back to Kelton. Foreign talk and train whistle lessened in his head. "But it's too late now to go today. We'll have to start out in the morning. I guess I've got time to get back for evening milking."

Matthew hobbled into the barn and dodged the swinging tail of a cow.

Pa glanced up at him. "You're late, son. What were you and Josh up to?"

Matthew forced a smile. "Sorry, I'm so slow."

He shoved his hands in his pockets. Chinese babbling echoed softly all around him. He shook his head. *Craziness.*

"Peterson said he saw you and Josh heading out to the desert. Wish I knew what was going on in your head."

No you don't, thought Matthew, picturing the ghost train, smoke billowing from the steam engine, light swaying in the distance. *Good thing Pa can't see it. He would know I'm crazy.*

"I'll start with the Jersey." He pulled her into the stall, crouched on the three-legged stool—his leg out to the side—and cleaned her teats.

Pa shook his head and pitched a forkful of hay for the cow to munch.

That night at dinner Mother ruffled Matthew's hair. "Had a good day? I hear you and Josh were exploring the desert."

"Word gets around." Matthew glanced up at Pa. "Seems everyone knows my business."

"I saw that look," said Mother. "I know you're growing up, and I can't watch you every minute. I just want to keep you safe. Now that Cassie's gone, you're all I have."

Guilt tightened Matthew's gut. What would she do if he wasn't there? Maybe he couldn't live up to Mother's expectations. Was he responsible for keeping her happy?

Matthew's thoughts turned to Dove Creek, and he heard the cry of the train whistle again. Was it the real train this time? He couldn't tell.

His mother sighed. "Sometimes I think I hear the sound of a train."

"What?" Matthew jerked his head up. Maybe he got his crazies from his mother.

She put her hand on his shoulder. "Somehow it's comforting." She let her fingers trail across his back. "Sounds silly doesn't it?"

Matthew helped her clear the dishes from the table.

Pa put his arm around Mother. "I'll wash, you dry," he said to Matthew. He kissed his wife's forehead.

"Your mother needs a rest. She hung all the wash on the line, and you know that hurts her back."

"Sure, Pa." Matthew hobbled to the sink.

The next morning Matthew turned the cows back into the pasture just as the sun climbed into the sky.

Josh swung the pasture gate open and shut it behind him. "Bad news."

"What?"

"I went to get the buckboard, but the hotel needs it today to get a load of flour from the mill."

"What about tomorrow?"

"We can take it today—late afternoon when the hotel's through using it," said Josh.

"That's great. Better timing anyway." Matthew slapped the rump of the last cow into the pasture, lifted the gate closed, and turned to leave. "We'll get there at night. Maybe we will hear the Chinks and see the train." Noise started in his head again.

"Don't count on it," said Josh.

"I'll tell Pa I want to spend the night with you," said Matthew. "He said he'd do the milking himself tonight. So we'll have until daybreak to get back."

"Good plan," said Josh.

With the sun sinking low in the sky, Matthew glanced behind him as Josh headed the buckboard out of town. "Wonder who's watching us? Somebody'll report to Pa."

"You're paranoid," said Josh.

"Not really. Last time we went, Peterson told Pa he saw us heading into the desert."

The horse clopped along, bouncing the wagon over the ruts in the road. Matthew hated buckboards. *They are purposefully built to shake every bone in my body.*

Josh was quiet—just looking toward the distant hills ahead.

Babbling began again in Matthew's head, but this time the voices sounded louder and angry. He hummed the tune "Oh Susanna" to get the sound to go away. Instead the noise grew louder. An image of an angry Chinese mob flickered just behind his eyes. Could he see it? Sort of. He glanced up at the sky to get the picture to go away. A cloud passed overhead, looking like a fat Chinaman with a long braid down his back. *I am nutty*, Matthew thought.

The sunset flamed with an orange glow.

"The sky looks like it's ablaze," said Matthew. *I wish a fire would burn those Chinks out of my head.*

"Pretty," said Josh.

"Not pretty." Matthew covered his ears with his hands. "Dangerous. I've got this ringing in my head, and I'm trying to get rid of it."

"What?"

"Oh, never mind," Matthew spat at a prairie dog that scampered along the ground.

"What's ailing you?" Josh stared at him. "You're becoming Mr. Sourness again."

Matthew dug his fingers into his bum leg. "I'm just in a bad mood." He could still see the crowd of Chinese workers in his mind, but this time they were shouting something and carrying knives. Matthew shook his head again, but the vision and the sound remained.

As they neared the steep grade to the camp, the voices became louder and angrier. Large knives pierced the air. *Maybe it wasn't a good idea to come up here.*

Darkness replaced dusk, and stars salted the sky.

They reached what remained of the ghost camp near the rail line. A scattering of pots and kitchen utensils gave evidence of the former inhabitants.

A light wind blew. It wasn't cold, but Josh shivered and rubbed his arms with his hands. "I ... I don't know if this is such a good idea."

"Are you chicken?" The noise in Matthew's head was becoming unbearable.

"Yeah," said Josh. "Maybe I am."

"Well, I'm not," Matthew said. He had to put on a good front. But he felt chicken. No, smaller than that. He felt like a robin about to be plucked out of the air by a hawk.

"Let's go back," said Josh.

"No!" Matthew stumbled down from the buckboard into the black night and hobbled toward the tracks. The angry crowd in his head seemed to overtake him. He ran to stay ahead of them. They screamed in his ears.

"Wait," called Josh. "I'm coming."

But Matthew didn't care. He couldn't be bothered with Josh. He had his own problems. Flying. He needed to fly away from the mob in his head.

In the distance he could see the tiny flicker of a light and could hear a faint train whistle. This time it was outside his head. *Hurry, hurry!* he thought. The knives flashed around him.

What was happening? He needed to get on that ghost train and away from the mob. But what about his mother? She would miss him. Both of her children gone. What about Pa? *I need to stay and help Pa.*

Matthew ducked to avoid the knives. He could feel the workers' breath on his neck. *This is stupid*, he thought. He crumpled to his knees. "Stop!" he shouted at the Chinese. They didn't listen.

The sound of the train came closer and closer. The mob pushed him into the ground. Matthew could smell the dust on their clothes and feel their greasy hands on his throat.

"Get up!" yelled Josh.

The train barreled closer.

"I can't," wailed Matthew. A knife gashed his shoulder. Blood. A fist belted the back of his head and flattened him onto the ground.

"Get up!" screamed Josh.

Matthew looked up. The train light blinded him and the blare of the horn drowned out the mob. He'd never get on the train now. It would pass him by, and he'd be killed by an angry mob in his head. *Crazy!*

A hand reached out and grabbed him. "Come on, Brother. Get up off the ground. This clickety-clacker won't slow for nothin."

Matthew felt himself being lifted into the air and pulled along.

Matthew turned. "Cassie!" His breath caught. "How come you're on this train?"

"Waitin' for you, Brother. Waitin' for you." She laughed. "You always did need rescuin.'"

The wind blew Matthew's hair from his face, drying the sweat on his forehead.

A distant scream. "No!" It was Josh.

"Tell Mother I'm fine." Matthew called to the air. He hugged his sister. "Cassie and I are fine."

Matthew grinned. "We're flyin.'"

The Upper Ogden Valley *in Utah sits at an elevation of just over 5,000 feet ensuring plentiful winter snow and comfortable summer temperatures. It is located 10 miles from Ogden City and 50 miles from Salt Lake City International Airport. It is a place of wide-open spaces, mountains, wetlands, rivers, gurgling mountain streams and the scenic Pineview Reservoir. Three towns are located in the valley, Huntsville, Eden and Liberty and there are three ski resorts in the surrounding mountains—Powder Mountain, Snowbasin and Wolf Mountain.*

5. Starry, Starry Night

Sherry Hogg

The night I died, there was a ring around the
moon.

*Crazy Aunt Sadie used to tell anyone who would
listen to count the stars between the moon and its
ring 'cause rain would be coming in that many days.
Trying like Jesus to hold my face above the almost
freezing water, I was counting those stars as fast as I
could and got to twelve just as I slipped under. The
lake closed quickly over my view like a glass panel,
opaque and final, and the bright moon with all its
stars slid away with everything else that was my life.
Legs beating, arms circling frantically, murky
Pineview water seeping into my lungs, I felt the
unmanageable weight of all my hurtful wrongdoings*

and willful indiscretions dragging me to the bottom like a heavy bag of stones.

***

They don't serve you at the Shooting Star Saloon—you belly up and order your own, so I did. "Get me a pitcher of Bud and a Star Burger to soak it up with," I told Sally the barkeep.

"Get it yourself," she shot back, pulling an empty pitcher from the stack. "What the hell are you doing up here on a Wednesday night? Wait, let me guess... blow in on a week day, order a pitcher for one... sounds like wifey trouble to me!"

I snorted to let her know how wrong she was. Neither one of us was convinced.

"Shows how much *you* know," I said. "It's taco night at the Legion. I only came over here 'cause I couldn't get in the parking lot over there... seems people actually like *their* grub!"

"Watch your mouth, I'll sic Buck on you," Sally warned, slamming down the pitcher and mug and motioning to the incredibly large St. Bernard head mounted forlornly on the wall facing the bar.

"I know, I know, and don't ask for fries... I got it. Just bring me that burger when you're done torturing it," I added with a wink, grabbing the beer and heading to the back.

I took our usual booth facing the pool table and poured myself a cold one. As the soothing stream of cool liquid comfort made its way to my gut, I replayed the events of the past hour in my mind.

Being ambushed in the driveway by an angry wife was the least of it. Ellen couldn't possibly have known when she came barreling out the front door arms waving, jabbing angrily at her wrist, screaming that I wasn't the only son of a bitch on the planet, why didn't I ever consider anyone else's time or plans or feelings?—she had no way of knowing that I had just experienced one of the worst days in the history of me, and that piling this on top of everything else might be the proverbial last straw. Ellen didn't know and she didn't care.

Remembering that the .45 was stashed handily in the hallway closet, I pictured a messy murder-suicide as the inevitable end to this really crappy day. No need to subject our boys to that, I reasoned, dodging a flying spatula. Leaving the car in the driveway, ducking in the garage, jumping on my bike, and backing out seemed like a very logical alternative, so that's exactly what I did. Head down, finger up, I rode away and the shrill, shrieking volume of my wife's very righteous rage faded into the evening air.

Before I knew where I was going, I was halfway up the canyon. Feeling the Vincent under me, leaning into the curves, blasting through the crisp mountain air, I felt somewhat righted and relieved. I took the Narrows recklessly, accelerating into the tightness of each turn. Entering the last curve, I bumped the throttle and felt the back tire slip as the sheer rock cliffs crowded the bike toward the rushing river. *Good*, I thought, *this can be it*. What better way to go than riding a '59 Vincent Comet straight through a curve?

Except—I didn't want to die. Not really. Not today. And I really didn't want to mess up the custom paint job my dad had been so proud of. *This is a damn good bike*, I reminded myself. *And you have good boys at home. They all deserve better*. By the time the road crossed the river at *Gray Cliff* I had eased up on the throttle and was having a look at the moon. It was a good one... three-quarters full, threading in and out of some high, wispy clouds.

Pineview dam loomed just ahead and as I climbed the final grade past it, the water rose into view. A bright trail of beckoning light stretched out on the lake's surface from the reflected moon, and I wished for a moment I could ride out on it. The path looked that straight and steady.

Across the water, the twinkling lights of Huntsville reminded me that a Star Burger and pitcher were just minutes away, and probably exactly what I needed to calm my jagged nerves. Ten minutes later I was sitting at our table, staring up at the ceiling full of dollar bills, each one signed by people who had definitely been having a much better time than me.

Feeling all alone and like I probably deserved it, I took another swig and hollered in the kitchen for my burger. The door swung open and Sally's hand appeared with a basket. I grabbed it, grunted a thanks and she disappeared. Some tourists had just come in and she was wanted up front. Quarters for the jukebox and a history of Huntsville—these were Sally's least favorite requests. They wanted both.

Three delicious bites into the soul-warming concoction that is a Star Burger, I heard the quarters drop. Soon Neil Young was crooning "Heart of Gold," filling the room with a sweet '70s vibe that suited my mood just fine. I laid my head back and closed my eyes, feeling the burger and beer and the old music transport me back to a simpler time. A time before kids, before responsibility, before my wife wanted to decapitate me with a kitchen utensil.

When I opened my eyes, there was a girl at the back of the room I hadn't seen before. She was sitting in the corner booth, looking like someone had shoved her there. In the dim light, I could make out a set of finely shaped features, pale and small, emerging from a mass of unruly red hair that had the curious effect of being completely seductive. Her tiny face was mostly taken up by a pair of unfittingly large eyes that from a distance looked like reflecting pools, and I wanted to get a closer look to see just what was in them.

Picking up my pitcher and a mug from the sideboard, I approached the girl and her booth. A bit unsteady, but with bravado I had picked up somewhere in the middle of my third glass, I slid onto the bench across from her.

"My name is Sam. Can I buy you a drink? Oh look, I already have," I said setting down the pitcher and mug.

She seemed entirely homemade—a coarse linen shirt dress, too light for the late fall weather, muted wool shawl draped crookedly over her slight shoulders. On the floor next to her feet sat a soiled knapsack, fashioned from a small cotton shirt. Sleeves tied across the bundle provided a handle and easy access to its contents.

She lifted her head to have a look at me. I had been right about the eyes—they were bottomless, dark, and eerily empty. She seemed to be reading my soul and looking straight through me at the same time. After several moments of intense study, she still hadn't spoken and I began to wonder what the hold-up was.

"You have something against beer?" I queried. "Funny way to show it, hanging out in a bar."

Her eyes spoke before she did. They told me to go away. But looking straight in them, I got lost and felt a bit like drowning, so I continued to babble.

"You look cold. I can help you with that." Leaning forward in my seat, I yelled, "Sally, get me another burger!" There was no sign from the front that Sally heard me, or was even in the building, so I moved to get up.

The girl's tiny hand darted forward and touched mine. It felt like a small piece of ice nestling on my skin. Her voice was low and sweet, with an accent I couldn't place, something country. "Never mind, I can't eat, but thank you. I'm not hungry, that is. I just—" Her voice trailed off and something in me twitched. I couldn't stand not knowing what she had almost said.

"Look, if you're not hungry, have a drink," I said, pouring her one. "What's your name, anyway?

You're from the valley, right? Huntsville? Eden? I know I've seen you around."

She pulled her hand away from mine, retreating from the barrage of questions and shot me a glance. I was infinitely happy to get a look in those eyes again. They were the exact color of the lake just after the sun leaves it—both green and blue, but mostly just dark. And they were full of something like unfathomable sorrow or soul wrenching regret so that looking in them made you know she was broken. It made me want like hell to fix her.

"Please," I begged, completely lost in the beer and the night and her eyes, "tell me something about yourself. Something. Anything."

Shrugging in grudging surrender, she told me her name was Molly and she lived "over there," gesturing vaguely north-northeast, which could have meant Woods Market, the highway, or South Fork, depending on how far you thought she was pointing.

"Well, Molly from Over There," I said, standing up unsteadily and out of the booth, "you don't eat or drink but how do you feel about dancing?" I held out my hand, fully expecting her to shoot me another scathing look. Instead she smiled and jumped up, brushing past me like a gust of wind. Miss Molly was in a mood to dance and the jukebox seemed eager to oblige.

The next thirty minutes passed in a whirl of hillbilly two-steps and old-timey waltzes. Molly did almost all the dancing herself, twirling and spinning around me as if I were a useful post with arms. Occasionally she'd grab one and spin out to the end of it and back in, snuggling up against me. I was just drunk enough to love the feel of her cool slenderness pressed up against me. As my hand slipped to her waist, I envisioned Ellen standing in the driveway with the spatula and took a quick step back.

"Mind if we sit this one out?" I suggested, "I need a drink." What I really needed was not to be standing so close to her, or touching her, or watching her body move in that thin cotton dress. Where was the painfully shy and melancholy girl of an hour ago? She had seemed to need fixing—had I fixed her? Now I was the one that needed saving.

"Oh, but I love this one!" Molly cried, grabbing both my hands, and sashaying backwards onto the floor, pulling me with her. "'Buffalo Gals won't you come out tonight and dance by the light of the moon,'" she crooned, eyes closed, hips swaying.

"Lordy, lordy," she murmured happily. "I'm so glad I stepped in here, you're really the sweetest fella," She lifted her face to mine.

I was almost irretrievably lost in those bottomless eyes when they brightened suddenly. "Say, I have a wonderful idea!" she cried, turning toward the front door and tugging on my hand, "Let's go dance by the light of the moon! It's such beautiful night! I know a place down by the water. We might even jump in if we feel like it."

I hesitated, trying to calculate how drunk I was. Drunk enough to sashay and skinny-dip with a beautiful red-headed stranger in the light of a three-quarter moon? I decided I was just that drunk. Besides, I rationalized, if there was anything I could use right now, it was a breath of fresh air and a cool splash of water. *Clear my head for the ride home*, I thought.

We were almost to the front door when Molly remembered her knapsack. "Oh, just a sec... I never go anywhere without that!" she said, heading back to the table. I leaned over the bar and yelled into the kitchen at Sally. "I'm outta here lady—thanks for the grub." She stepped out from behind the kitchen curtain, wiping her hands on a towel. "All right then, don't be a stranger. I'd hate to try to make it through Taco Night without you—gets pretty lonely over here, you know. Ride safe."

"If you say so," I shrugged. "See you in a couple of weeks—if you didn't give me food poisoning, that is." I opened the front door and Molly ran past me, out the open door, and into the night. Stepping into the crispness of an ending fall, I let the heavy wood door slam shut behind me and turned to face my little hitchhiker. By moonlight, she looked like little more than a ghostly wisp of smoke or vapor, but I knew that was an illusion. Hadn't I spent the last half-hour spinning the girl around a dance floor, charming her with my wit and humor, and trying like hell to keep from kissing her? She was real, alright. She was real or I was bat-crap crazy.

"Where to, woman?" I asked, hoping with everything in me that the spot Molly had in mind was not the beach at Cemetery Point. But sure enough, she raised a pale arm and pointed in that direction. Trying to ignore the knot that was tying itself up in my stomach, I threw a leg over the bike and motioned her to climb on. Molly wrapped her arms around my waist and snuggled tightly into my back. Heading west on First Street, I felt like I was wearing a coat of ice. *When we get there, I'm giving this girl my jacket*, I thought. *She could use some warming up.*

Five minutes later we reached the cemetery, rode past the empty guard shack, and arrived at the beach. The cottonwoods at the water's edge were almost bare, and the crooked branches stretched into the sky like craggly old witches' fingers reaching for the moon. We gathered up some dry leaves and deadwood. I pulled out my lighter, and soon the small pile was giving off a comforting crackle with a wispy trail of smoke. We sat cross-legged next to it, warming our hands and anything else we could get some heat on.

I glanced at Molly. Her tiny face, by fire and moonlight was pale and pinched looking. The lightness and joy of earlier had faded with the music and lights of the saloon. Sorrow and loss had returned, and emptiness. I needed to understand.

"What's your story, Miss Molly? I like to know a bit about the girls I take for a turn under the moon." Her eyes were fixed with a laser gaze out on the lake and the watery moonlit trail. I tried again. "Married? Children?"

She gave a slight nod, a flicker of something like life in her eyes. I knew I was pushing it out of bounds now, but I needed to know. "Where are they?"

Reaching in the knapsack, Molly pulled out a small piece of worn paper, creased and yellow, covered with old-fashioned news print. I squinted to make out the ancient headline, "Man Sinks Boat in Lake, All Lost."

The article described the drowning of a man and his two sons. Despondent over the infidelity of his young wife, the man had rowed a wooden skiff to the middle of the lake and sunk it, babies and all. The newspaper was dated Sept. 27, 1946.

Molly turned her face to mine, and for the first time I truly comprehended the depth of her unfathomable eyes. They didn't *seem* bottomless and empty. They *were* bottomless and empty.

A shiver of actual terror traversed my spine as she rose slowly to her feet. Her arm lifted slowly as if pulled by a string, floating up from her body, finger extended toward the vast shimmering emptiness that was the lake. Turning her head slowly back to meet my horrified gaze, she seemed a luminous specter of grief and despair.

I glanced furtively up to the pavement where the bike was parked and imagined myself jumping on it and roaring out of there, away from the water, away from the moon, and away from this poor delusional girl who obviously needed much more help than I could possibly give her. However, I realized that if I did leave Molly here, trailing her shawl on the beach, any investigation would reveal that I was the person she had ridden away into the night with—the last person to see her alive. I'd watched way too many crime dramas to think that would turn out well for me.

As I turned back to the beach, my heart jumped. A trail of footprints stretched out from the circle of firelight to the water's edge, and I could make out the outline of Molly's head and shoulders emerging from the lake about a dozen feet from shore. Sprinting the length of the beach down to the water, I called her name, hoping like hell to break the spell or trance or whatever was pulling her out into that watery trail of moonlight. She made no response, and I watched with horror as the white fabric of her shoulders sank under the lake's surface till all that was left in view was the tiny face, drawn and pale, a mass of red hair floating all around it.

Unhesitating, I dove in and resurfaced a short distance from her. Her eyes—calm, peaceful, and serene—met mine, sending a chill of fear and dread racing through my body. I reached frantically under the water for her hand, arm, or any part of her I could latch onto and use to pull her up to safety. There was nothing there. Slowly her sweet little face slipped underwater, eyes open, hair trailing, disappearing slowly into the murky darkness of the lake as if she belonged there and was simply going home.

Diving down, searching desperately for a sign of her, I began to feel the cold seeping through my heavy clothing, chilling my skin and flesh, and moving right into my bones. Coming up for a quick gasp of air, and then back down again, I began to entertain the possibility that she was gone—that I had lost her—that I really was going to be the last person to see her alive. I couldn't let that happen.

Twisting and turning under the water, I strained my eyes for a glimpse of trailing fabric, a frail arm reaching upward, or any sign of life in the impenetrable, frigid darkness. Finally I caught a glimpse of something falling away, making a swift descent to the faraway bottom of the lake. It was Molly's knapsack, sleeves untied and trailing. Pouring from the bottom of the open shirt—a child's shirt—was a cascade of stones. The bundle was visible for less than a moment and then gone, with every other trace of the beautiful girl, her sorrow, and her story.

I returned choking and shivering to the surface of the lake. Looking frantically toward the almost invisible shore, I suddenly realized I was going to drown. Weighted down with my clothes and the freezing water, and feeling disoriented, still a little drunk, and completely exhausted, I saw no way of making it across the hundred feet of frigid water that stretched like an icy grave between the shore and me.

Treading water would buy me five minutes at best, I realized, and so I turned my gaze upward to the brightly ringed moon and began counting stars.

Mount Ogden, *at 9,570 feet, is part of the northern Wasatch Range in Weber County, UT. It towers over downtown, Ogden. It has numerous hiking trails. Ogden lies on its East side and the Ogden Valley with the scenic Pineview Reservoir, on the West. The summit features several large radio towers and a helipad. Mount Ogden is home to Snowbasin ski resort, where the 2002 Olympics were held.*

PHOTO COURTESY FENTRESS-BRADBURN ARCHITECTS - DENVER

6. Dancing to the Stars

Barbara Emanuelson

"We're here, Mama!" Elizabeth called out as she rushed ahead of her mother on Washington Boulevard. Brenda could barely keep up with her energetic fourth grader.

"Hold up, there, Butterfly," Brenda said, huffing and puffing as she made her way up the busy street to get to Peery's Egyptian Theatre.

Elizabeth loved and adored this old place. They'd learned at the dance studio that Peery's Egyptian was built in 1924 as a premiere movie palace in the heart of downtown Odgen. They'd almost torn it down in the 1980s, but instead, it was restored and made into this amazing structure that Elizabeth and her friends were going to get to dance in for everyone to see.

"Wait for me, sweetie," Elizabeth's mom said with a chuckle. They were greeted by the elderly theatre manager, Mr. Grady, the dance teacher, Miss Julie, and a throng of other little dancers and their moms.

"Get in place with your class," Miss Julie instructed. "See you in two plus hours, moms. We should be finished by around eight-thirty or so."

Several dance classes were coming together in the historic location for the yearly recital. The grand performance would be the culmination of many hours of training, studying moves, and practicing routines for friends and family to see. Assembling in the refurbished vestibule, the students gathered in clumps and headed past the concession stand with Miss Julie at the front of the pack. Elizabeth waved as her mom left the theatre.

The dancers chitter-chattered as they stepped into the theatre. Centuries seemed to vanish before their eyes as they left the modern world behind and sunk into their seats, gazing in awe at the Egyptian sculptures and hieroglyphic columns on either side of the stage. Row by row, the children's voices hushed as the adult volunteers guided them to their assigned seats. Miss Julie stood on the columned stage smiling down at the rows and rows of her charges, a bright smile on her serene face. The children looked adoringly up at their beloved teacher.

"Welcome, all of you. Thank you for coming in so nicely. You did a great job getting right to your seats. I want to thank my parent volunteers for taking time out of their busy schedules to get everyone here on time. I know it's going to be Mother's Day on Sunday and I appreciate that you're going to spend it here for your child's dance recital. We have two rehearsal days, so let's make the most of them. Let's all remember to sit exactly where you are right now. Look at who's on either side of you. This is the same order you'll be in when you go on stage. Be here at two tomorrow for full dress rehearsal. That way, any issues with costumes can be addressed. Please remember to *bring* your ballet shoes. Do NOT wear them on the street! Shake your heads to let me know you understand."

Seventy-five heads of every size and color bobbled affirmation toward the beautiful dancer on stage. She smiled and met their happy gazes with a clap of her hands.

"Let's get started." She peered down at the hand raised in fourth row. "What is it, Elizabeth?"

Elizabeth pointed to her left. "Savannah's not here, Miss Julie. She's my partner for our dance."

"I know, honey. Her mama called me and said she was getting over a stomach bug. She'll be here tomorrow, though. Just pretend she's here when you go on stage, okay?"

Elizabeth nodded. She'd try to remember to leave space for her friend to fill during the actual recital.

Excitement filled the air. It was as much a feeling of anticipation as it was a sense of otherworldliness in the theatre. Antiquity and modern were married with each glinting star near the lighted windows and boxes up top. The hieroglyphs on the frieze above the stage and on the side columns beckoned everyone to a place beyond yesteryear. Eons melted before their eyes as each class waited to dance on the stage.

It wasn't merely the appearance of the unique theatre, though; it was the way it smelled, too. Faint scents of popcorn, oil paint, and varnish all mixed together with the memories of movies, orchestras, and other dancers who'd performed here; opening a window into a time long past. Music filled the air as the dancers began their movement.

Elizabeth watched in awe as the first group began their Egyptian folk dance. The song played an ancient cadence, setting the tone for the program of both old and new. Elizabeth closed her eyes, taking in the multi-sensory experience. She imagined herself as a young girl in ancient Egypt, dressed in a gown of white with gold bangle bracelets up and down her arms, swaying with the papyrus plants and grasses on the banks of the Nile River.

Suddenly, a girl's voice startled her out of her reverie.

"That dancing is the cat's meow!"

Elizabeth turned toward her left to see who sat down in Savannah's empty seat. "What?"

The young girl bounced in her seat. "The girls on stage. They really are good."

Elizabeth nodded. "Yeah, they are." She'd never seen this girl before, but she could be joining them from another dance class. "Hey, what number are you in? The Charleston?"

The girl tossed her long, blonde curls over her shoulder. "What do you mean?"

Instead of responding, Elizabeth still marveled at the girl's outfit. "Your costume is great, but you weren't supposed to be wearing it today, you know?"

"What costume?" the girl asked, cocking her head to the side.

"Your dress, silly," Elizabeth noted with a giggle. "It's such a pretty blue color." It had a long satin sash that hung low and matched the small bow in the girl's long, curly, blonde hair. Glancing down, Elizabeth noted, "And your shoes! How are you going to dance in those things? Do the laces hurt?"

"Nah, I'm used to them," she replied, looking down at the stiff black shoes.

"I mean, they're so tight over the top of your foot and all the way up your ankles."

"I wear them all the time," the girl noted.

Elizabeth wrinkled her nose. Miss Julie wasn't going to be happy with those shoes. She hoped the girl had her ballet slippers with her, as well. The girl didn't seem to care, though, as she sat in awe watching the rehearsal.

"I don't remember seeing you before. I'm Elizabeth. What's your name?"

"Oh, I've been here all day," the girl said nonchalantly. "I'm here a lot because my daddy works here."

"He does? My dad works at a church. What's your name?"

"Alison. But, my daddy calls me Nutter-butter because I love peanut butter sandwiches. I brought him one for lunch today."

Elizabeth giggled. "My daddy calls me Monkey because I love to climb. My mom calls me Butterfly because I love to spin around and dance."

Both girls snickered, holding their hands over their mouths as the people in front of them twisted around to stare.

"*Sh-h-h-h,*" hissed Elizabeth's friend, Bella, sitting on her right. "You better be quiet or you'll get in trouble. Who were you talking to anyway?"

"Alison," she said to her friend. Bella furrowed her brows. "Who?"

Elizabeth turned to the empty seat on her left. With a shrug, she said, "Oh... never mind. I guess she had to get ready to go up on stage."

Before she knew it, it was their turn to go. "This way, girls," Bella's mom said, ushering them backstage. "Remember to stay in place."

The line of nine little dancers filed behind her through the entrance door to backstage. As the girls waited, they watched the older group perform their pointe routine to Tchaikovsky's *Swan* Lake excerpt. Bella and Elizabeth joined hands and began twirling to the music until Bella's mom snapped her fingers to get their attention. They widened their eyes as they took their places once more, waiting to dance.

However, across the stage, in the wings, stood Alison. She smiled at Elizabeth and waved at her. Elizabeth waved back. Beethoven's *Für Elise* filled the air as each girl fell into choreographed rhythm.

Miss Julie's voice could be heard as she called from the first row. "Stay together, girls. Better... good... keep your line straight."

As promised, Miss Julie had the girls finished with their rehearsal by eight-thirty. Brenda was waiting in the vestibule for her Elizabeth. They held hands as they left the theatre.

"How'd it go?" Brenda asked as Elizabeth got into their Mercury minivan.

"Good, Mama! It was a lot of fun. Isn't the theatre cool?"

"Very. I've never seen anything like it," she said, crooking her head to make sure Elizabeth was buckled in before driving.

"I'm hungry, Mama. Can we stop on the way home?"

"Sure. How about a hamburger or something?" Brenda suggested. "We can go to the McDonald's near Acres."

"Yay! Can we eat there? Please?"

"Okay," said Brenda, not too enthusiastically steering toward the fast food haven.

After parking, ordering, and taking a seat, Elizabeth took a bite of her cheeseburger, savoring the pickles. "Yum."

"Glad it's hitting the spot."

"Why aren't you eating, Mama?"

"Because Daddy had a meeting at church and we ate early. I'm good with my soda," she said, lightly pinching her daughter's nose.

"I made a new friend tonight. Her name is Alison and she said her daddy works there. It was weird, though, because she was already wearing her costume tonight."

Brenda reached across and snagged a French fry. "Oh, yeah? I thought dress rehearsal was tomorrow."

"It is. I guess she got it mixed up. Anyway, she's really nice. I like meeting girls from the other dance classes."

"Good, I'm glad. Finish up now. It's getting late. You need to get a bath before you get ready for bed."

Elizabeth hurried to finish up her food. "Okay, Mommy."

***

The next day—dress rehearsal day—Elizabeth twirled and spun around in the living room in her flowing pink costume. As Brenda gathered her purse and keys, Elizabeth kissed her father goodbye and followed her mother out to the car.

"See you later, Monkey. Be careful not to mess up that pretty costume," her dad said as he closed the minivan door behind her. He waved as they pulled out of the driveway.

Elizabeth turned back to her mother. "Can Alison come over today?"

"Well, honey, since I haven't met her, I'd have to talk to her parents first. They don't know us. I'll try to touch base with her mother and father. Point her out to me, and we'll go say hello. How's that sound?"

"Great! Are you staying today, Mama?"

"No, baby, I'm not. I'm one of the performance day mommies. I'll be back stage on Sunday." Her mom steered to the right toward the theatre. "Almost there. Be good, now, and make sure to follow directions. Don't go exploring."

Elizabeth couldn't stop herself from reacting. "*Mooooom...*"

"Don't roll your eyes at me, young lady. We both know how you love to do your own thing. Or, did you forget about Dawn and David's wedding last month? Climbing out the window at the castle reception hall in Layton? Do you think the fire department enjoyed having to send their men up that ladder and put a big parachute underneath in case you fell?"

"No, Mama," she said as she pouted. "I said I was sorry."

"I'm glad of it, but I can't say I enjoyed the experience. It's a good thing Dawn has a sense of humor."

"Too bad you don't," whispered Elizabeth, barely audibly.

"*What was that?*" her mother said, as she pulled in front of the theatre. Brenda turned with a flick of the head. She raised her eyebrows. "I mean it, Lizzie."

"Okay, okay! Please, can I go?"

"Yes. See you around four. I'll come inside and watch. Maybe you can introduce me to your friend then."

"Bye, Mama," she said as she got out of the van.

Brenda waved as Elizabeth joined the melee of other little girls. "Remember what I said, Lizzie," she called out as the girls headed into the theatre.

Elizabeth did mostly as her mother had admonished, but she walked around hoping to see Alison. When the Charleston class got on stage, Elizabeth scanned the group, one girl at a time, as they danced in time to the happy music. Where was Allison? Perhaps she was backstage or in the wings? Elizabeth twisted around, trying to see past the curtains. There are so many people from the studio, but no sign of her new friend. She frowned at the thought and let out a long sigh.

Slumping back into her seat, she turned to Bella and asked, "Remember the girl I was talking to yesterday? Alison, I mean. Have you seen her?"

"I never saw her yesterday, Elizabeth."

Incredulous, Elizabeth snapped, "Sure you did. She was in Savannah's seat."

Bella tossed her head about and then gave Elizabeth a weird look. "Was she? I don't know where she is. I don't even know *who* she is."

The theatre manager, Mr. Grady, appeared and crouched down next to them in the aisle. There was the hint of a laugh in his kindly old face when he said, "It's quiet time. What are you girls talking about?"

Bella said, "Some girl named Alison, Mr. Grady. Elizabeth's friend."

The man's features went slack. "W-w-who's Elizabeth?" he asked shakily.

"I am. I met Alison yesterday. She was really nice. Pretty, too. She said her dad works here. Do you know them?"

The elderly man's face blanched. "What'd she look like?"

"Blonde hair with curls down to here," she said, gesturing toward her shoulders.

He blinked hard and swallowed. "What was she wearing?"

"A blue costume and hard, high-up shoes, not ballet shoes," Elizabeth explained.

He stared at the ground and shook his head. "No...no, I don't imagine they were. Where'd you see her?"

"Next to me in my dance partner's seat... over there," Elizabeth said, pointing to her left.

The elderly man grabbed onto the armrest and clumsily pulled himself up. He trembled in place for a moment and then, without another word, he hurried up the aisle and out of the theatre.

The girls glanced at each other quizzically. "Did I say something wrong?" Elizabeth asked.

"Maybe Mr. Grady is that Alison girl's grandpa," Bella said.

"Yeah, he probably just went to look for her or something." Elizabeth shrugged and let out another sigh.

***

At a quarter to four that afternoon, Brenda was seated toward the back of the theatre. She moved closer in when Miss Julie came out to talk to the parents.

"Don't forget to be here at one p.m., sharp tomorrow for the performance. What's the rule about ballet shoes, dancers?"

"Carry them, don't wear them," the children recited in chorus.

Elizabeth spotted her mother and ran up the aisle.

"Hi, honey. Where's your new friend? I'd love to meet her."

"I didn't see her today. No one did. I think her grandpa works here, though. He went to look for her." She stopped when she spotted Mr. Grady and pointed in his direction. "There he is, Mama."

Brenda took Elizabeth by the hand. "Let's go talk to him."

"I'm Elizabeth's mom," she said. "Elizabeth's been looking for your granddaughter, Alison. Is she here today?"

"No, no... I'm not her grandpa." He bent down to Elizabeth's level. "Look, are you sure you saw her, Elizabeth?"

"Honest, mister, I did. Can she come over my house?"

"No. No, she can't." He turned with such abruptness that it startled Elizabeth.

Her hand flew to her mouth and she stifled a gasp. "What did I do?"

Brenda's mouth dropped open and she gazed down at the pained expression on her child's face. "It's okay, honey. These people don't know us.

Although, I will say he was rather peculiar and a bit odd. Perhaps another one of your friends can come over."

Elizabeth felt her lip push forward into a pout. "But, I like Alison, Mama."

Taking a deep breath, Brenda said, "Tell you what. I'll try to talk to Mr. Grady again tomorrow, okay?"

Elizabeth nodded and followed her mother out of the theatre.

***

Recital day was a busy one with dancers of all ages scurrying around dressed in their dance finery as flappers, swans, ducklings, and spiders.

"Break a leg, Monkey. You'll be great," Elizabeth's father said as they left the back stage area to take their seat out front.

One by one, the dance classes performed to loud applause and ovations.

Soon, it was intermission. The lights turned on and Brenda walked seven rows down the aisle where Elizabeth's class sat. Her child's seat was empty.

"Bella, where's Elizabeth?"

"I don't know, Miss Brenda. I saw her go back there," she said, pointing to the door in the front section.

With a heavy sigh, Brenda went to find Elizabeth. The lights began to flicker on and off. People looked at each other, sat back down, and then stood up again. Brenda spun around quickly; her anxious gaze meeting her husband's questioning eyes. "Lizzie?" she mouthed.

He shrugged his shoulders.

The lights went out again and then back on. Then, there was screaming.

Brenda heard her child's name and turned with a start. "Elizabeth!"

"Oh, my God! Somebody help her! John!"

Elizabeth was hanging from one of the balcony boxes above the stage. The child was clutching the window railing as the crowd gasped. Elizabeth's father, John, pushed the throng out of the way. "Hold on, Lizzie! Daddy's coming!"

"How do I get up there?" he screamed out to anyone who would help.

Mr. Grady rushed to his aid. "This way. Follow me."

The old man stood at the door by the fourth row of seats. John followed him onto a narrow set of twenty steps. At the top, there was a small platform and an open door. Hurrying up the steps, he went to the old box, stepping around the seats until he saw the bare-knuckled hands of his daughter, clinging to life.

'I've got you, Monkey," he assured her, even though he wasn't so certain. He yanked her up over the rail to safety, taking her into his arms as she sobbed into his shoulder. "You're fine, baby. It's okay."

Safely down the steps now, they saw Brenda and the old man at the bottom.

"Whatever prompted you to do that, Elizabeth?" Brenda cried out frantically, yet relieved.

"Alison was up there. She waved at me to come up. So, I left my seat and did. It was dark up there. I couldn't see her, but I heard her."

"What did she say?" the old man asked, his voice obviously shaky.

"She told me, 'Look up at the stars! If you go to the edge and see into the back of the theatre, it looks like the stars they go on and on forever.' So, I did it and that's when I fell over the edge."

"It's a miracle you didn't fall to your death!" scolded her much-relieved but frantic mother.

Elizabeth shook her head and explained. "It was Alison. She caught me. She grabbed my arms and told me to hold on tight. She said she'd get someone's attention with the lights."

She watched as her parents and Mr. Grady traded shocked expressions.

Her father glanced around. "Where is she? I'd like to thank her for helping you."

Mr. Grady wiped a tear away from his left eye and released a guttural groan. "She's not here. At least, not really."

"What do you mean?"

Mr. Grady stood firm as he looked directly at Elizabeth. "She's been gone these seventy-seven years."

Elizabeth's eyes widened and she clasped her father's hand tightly.

The old man continued. "Alison was my big sister. She came here when our dad was working one day. She wandered up the steps into the box. It was all new back then, y'see. Oh, how she loved it here! She fell from that very window. It was 1923." Mr. Grady stopped for a moment to collect himself. Then, he said, "She must've really liked you, Elizabeth. I'm glad you're okay. You be careful from now on, ye hear me?"

He patted her on the shoulder, turned, and then slowly walked away with his head bent down.

Elizabeth and her parents were silent watching him leave them, as sadness enveloped the air. They wondered at what had happened, hugging each other and pondering the idea of a theatre specter here at the Egyptian. Relief flooded the minds of Elizabeth's parents.

But, for Elizabeth there was a singular thought: Alison was, indeed, a good friend. Ghost or not, she'd saved her life.

Ben Lomond Peak, *at 9,712 feet, lies just north of Ogden, Utah. It is probably the most famous of the peaks in the northern portion of the Wasatch Mountains. A popular trail passes over its summit. It was named after the mountain, Ben Lomond, in the Scottish Highlands. Paramount Pictures logo, known as Majestic Mountain, was modeled after Mount Ben Lomond. Native Ogdenite, William W. Hodkinson, the founder of Paramount, initially drew the image on a napkin during a meeting in 1914.*

7. The Girl Upstairs

Jodi Brown

D ark chocolate curls fell across the little
girl's forehead as she parted the curtains
and peered through the window. When the
moving truck pulled in, she jumped up clapping her
hands. "She's here! She's here!"

The bottom floor apartment may not have
appealed to some, but Sheila had lived in basements
all her life; it was clean, affordable, and the
neighborhood was decent. She stood in front of the
building—its name painted in block letters on a big

board displayed on the front lawn—MOUNTAIN VIEW APARTMENTS.

Sheila thought she heard laughter and glanced at the upstairs apartment window. A child's face framed in dark curls peered straight at her before the curtains fluttered shut.

What a cute little girl, she thought, heading down the stairs with a heavy box. She had told her husband, Mark, she'd be able to handle the last truckload by herself while he went to work and Joey was at school. The image of the girl stayed with her. *I wonder if that's what my little Abby looks like now*, she wondered, setting the box on the kitchen counter and heading back out for another. *It's been four years. She'd be about the same age.*

Sheila knew she shouldn't let her mind go there. But the innocent face behind the glass made it hard not to. Most of the time, she kept her mind on work so her thoughts didn't wander. But some sights, like this little girl, triggered emotions so powerful that it seemed they were rooted in memories, not just wishful dreams.

Sheila finished unloading the truck. *Time for a rest,* she thought. But just as she was about to put her feet up, she heard Joey's school bus pull up outside. She rushed out to make sure she would be there when he got off.

"How about we get a snack and do your homework before your dad comes home?"

"Okay," Joey said, letting Sheila help him with his backpack.

It's different this time, Sheila thought. *Me and Mark are gonna make it work, and I'm gonna be Joey's momma—a good momma. Not like with Abby.*

She was sure of it—but she'd been sure before.

Sheila's relationship with Joey was still awkward but she hoped it would improve when they got settled. Her new stepson was identical to his father, from his fair skin to his golden hair, which made Sheila vow to love him all the more. The counselor had said his shyness and trouble sleeping was due to emotional trauma after his parents split up.

"Who'd have thought we'd get an apartment like this?" Mark asked that night as they stood gazing out their bedroom window. "Our first real place together and we already have a nice big lawn, views of Ben Lomond Peak and Mount Ogden— we're going somewhere, I tell ya."

He backed away from the window, grabbed Sheila, and threw her playfully onto the bed. He buried his face in her neck and kissed behind her ear.

Sheila laughed nervously but sounded annoyed when she said, "Joey's in the next room!"

"Nah, he's out back playin' with a girl. I left the door open so we can hear 'em."

Sheila sat up. "The little girl above us?"

"I dunno. Little girl with dark hair."

"She lives upstairs and Joey's already nick-named her Curly," Sheila said. "She looks about the same age—"

"Ahh, now don't start that again. Can't we go a day without talkin' about her?" Mark asked resentfully.

"I know, I know—sorry," she said and quickly added, "I'm gonna finish up dinner."

Mark rolled off the bed and walked out to get Joey. Sheila went into the kitchen.

After dinner and giving Joey a bath, they tucked him in and wished him a good night. They were pleased to see him smile and snuggle into his comforter.

Back in their own room, Mark said, "Man, I thought he'd be too excited to sleep, but the kid's zonked. Must be worn out."

"And he seems happier already," Sheila said with a smile, "it's like he knows we're in a better place.

For another couple of hours Sheila and Mark unpacked. Suddenly they heard footsteps outside the bedroom door.

"Look," Sheila said, pointing to a shadow under the door, "Joey's up. I hope he hasn't had a nightmare, being in a new place and all."

Sheila crossed the room before Mark moved. She opened the door, but Joey wasn't there. She went down the hall and peeked in his room. He was asleep in his bed.

"That was weird. I swear he was there," Sheila said as she walked back into the room.

"It was probably just creaks in this ol' building. Don't worry 'bout it. I'm beat, let's go to bed," Mark said, and they climbed onto their old queen mattress, which Sheila had disguised with new sheets.

Sheila lay in bed and thought about the girl upstairs, then about her own daughter.

"Mark, I promise not to talk about it all night, but seeing that little girl, well, there's no way that's her, right? I mean, could she be Abby?

Mark exhaled and replied, "I don't know, hon, but I kinda figure you would see Abby in every little girl you find, especially since you said it was a local family that got her."

Sheila was silently thankful. She had never heard him talk that way about Abby. His usual responses made her storm off and cry for hours.

He's right. I see Abby in every little girl who looks remotely like my baby. What if the girl upstairs is Abby? There's room in my life—and heart—for her now. I'm not the same person who handed my baby to that woman at the hospital. Of course, it's too late now. She belongs to another family.

Sheila rolled over and cried quietly. *I didn't take care of her—I just cared about him. I thought Abby's dad would stay with me if I had his baby.*

Mark was silent, but he put his hand on her shoulder as she wept.

***

The next day Sheila went back to work, ordering inventory and hanging clothes at the Dress Barn, but she made sure she got home in time to meet the bus.

That night, Mark got home early.

"Hey, I saw Joey's little girlfriend today," he said, pecking Sheila on the cheek. "I parked out back and saw her through the window—and I know I shouldn't say it, but she does look like you. Her hair even looks like curly willow branches, just like yours," Mark said grinning and shaking his head. "Maybe you should find out more—just so you know." He raised his eyebrows and shrugged.

At bedtime, Sheila found herself again staring at the ceiling and listening to the pattering of footsteps.

"Mark, I'm gonna call the company that placed Abby."

"I knew you would, babe," he replied.

Sleep was setting in when a loud clang sounded in the hall. Sheila jumped out of bed and checked the hallway. Nothing.

"There are the strangest sounds here at night," she grumbled getting back into bed.

"Told ya, probably the pipes or floorboards," Mark said, rolling over on his other side.

As Sheila dozed off, she pictured the girl upstairs running alongside her, Mark, and Joey, all of them a family, together.

The bedroom door creaked open and Sheila sat up startled. She saw Joey and exhaled.

"Geesh, Joey, you scared me," she looked at Mark who was still asleep, earplugs in place.

"Curly's bored, can I go play upstairs?" Joey asked, rubbing his eyes.

"Wh-what?" Sheila stammered. Her voice was high and unsteady. "Joey, it's the middle of the night. You can play tomorrow."

"But she wants to play now, Momma," he insisted.

He called me Momma, Sheila thought. Then she shook her head to clear her mind. "Nobody wants to play now. It's the middle of the night. Come on," she said as she walked him back to his room. Minutes after returning to her room, she heard noises in the hall.

He's up again? She threw the comforter off and got up.

"Joey, get back into bed!" she said as she opened his door, trying to be quiet but firm.

"I am in bed, like you said before," Joey whined.

Sheila stared into the darkness and saw him, in bed, blankets tight around his chin. She looked around the room and sighed. "Sorry, Bud, I'm tired. I thought I heard you walking around. 'Night."

She turned back toward her bedroom and no sooner had she closed her door than she saw a small shadow traipse past on the other side.

She yanked the door open but again nothing. *What in the world is wrong with me?* Sheila thought as she returned to her room.

***

"I called the adoption place." Sheila blurted the minute Mark came home from work the next day. "They said they couldn't talk to me about that kind of case over the phone—I have to go in person. I'm seeing them on Wednesday," she finished, wringing her fingers and smiling anxiously at Mark.

He pulled Sheila to him and hugged her. "That's great, babe, at last you will know more."

***

Wednesday afternoon arrived and Sheila's nerves quelled her excitement. She felt sick but she had told Mark she was okay to go on her own. Now she regretted that, as she sat alone in the small waiting area of the Child Services office. She wished Mark was there to hold her hand.

The office door opened and Sheila jumped.

"Ms. Curtis?" the social worker asked, glancing around at the half-dozen faces waiting their turn.

Sheila stood up and followed her into an office. "Dillard—I'm Mrs. Dillard now, just got married."

"Ahh, congratulations then," the woman said. "Go ahead and take a seat," she motioned.

Sheila blew out a long, slow breath, wondering what was going to come next.

"Mrs. Dillard, with a closed adoption, once a child has been placed with new parents, the record is sealed and we cannot provide information to the biological parents about that child."

Sheila began wringing her fingers, staring at the manila folder the woman had on her desk. "But you said, if I came in person—"

The woman nodded. "Your daughter's record is no longer sealed," she said tapping the folder.

"Why—what does that mean?"

"I'm sorry to have to tell you this, Mrs. Dillard, but unfortunately, your daughter—she passed away about six months ago. She died in her sleep from a brain aneurysm. The doctor said there was nothing anyone could have done."

Sheila's hand flew to her mouth; tears welled in her eyes. All she could do was shake her head.

"I'm so sorry," the social worker repeated.

Sheila looked at the wall clock and blinked away the tears. Joey'd be back from school soon.

I have to be there for him. I promised.

"Th-Thank you—for telling me." She sputtered out the words as she stood to leave. The social worker placed her hand on Sheila's trembling shoulder, and then Sheila walked out of the office.

She sat on the steps as she waited for Joey. As soon as he hopped off the bus, she ran over and bundled him in her arms.

Sheila tried to speak, but couldn't.

Joey didn't break her embrace. When she finally released him, he let her hold his hand all the way into the kitchen. They sat at the small table while he had a pop tart and a cup of milk.

"I drew a picture of Curly today," Joey said, pulling a piece of yellow construction paper out of his backpack. "Wanna see?"

"For sure, Bud." Sheila smiled but her eyes clouded with tears.

Joey had used a brown crayon to draw lots of curls, brown eyes, and a big smile on the otherwise stick-like figure.

"It's beautiful," Sheila said.

"Can I go show it to her?"

"Yeah—okay."

Sheila lay on the couch and listened to Joey and Curly running upstairs.

Mark found her still on the couch when he arrived home that night. At the sight of him, a fresh wave of tears washed over her and between sobs she told him the news.

"I'm sorry, hon, so sorry." He scooped her in his arms and held her as she cried.

Later, exhausted from grief, Sheila sank into the cushions of the sofa and wanted to stay there forever but she had promised herself that she would never neglect Joey like she did her little girl, not even now. In the two days that followed, she operated on autopilot; fulfilling her duties. She got Joey off to school and went to work. At the end of her shift, she came home to wait for Joey, fed him, and helped him with his homework. She sat at the table and had dinner with Mark even though her heart was breaking.

During times she was alone, she hibernated from the world, rocking in her seat on the sofa, her head on her knees. She realized that even though she gave her baby away, she never really let her go. She carried her with her, in her heart and mind.

***

Saturday morning Sheila awoke overwhelmed by a sense of well-being. She walked outside, laid down in the grass, and let the sun shine on her face. She sat up when she heard footsteps.

It was their landlord, Larry, walking down the stairs from apartment one with buckets, paint tins, and brushes.

"Hi, how are you?" he asked.

Sheila stood up and walked over to him. "I'm okay," she said, realizing that for the first time in three days she actually might be.

"Good, are you settled yet?"

"Yeah, the apartment's nice and roomy," she replied.

"Happy to hear it." Larry nodded. "Well, glad that's done—finished painting apartment one."

Sheila frowned. "Did the family have to move out while you painted the apartment?"

"That apartment is vacant. Haven't had any luck renting it for almost six months now. Every other place is rented but that one. Thought a fresh coat of paint might do the trick."

Sheila's eyes opened wide. Her hands started to shake and she swayed forward.

"You okay, ma'am?" Larry asked, grabbing Sheila's arm to steady her.

"That can't be true," Sheila whispered. "There's a little girl—I've seen her—*we've* seen her and Joey *played* with her and we've heard footsteps upstairs, every night."

Larry looked at her and cleared his throat. He seemed embarrassed. "Yes, I've heard that before. Some residents say they've seen shadows and heard footsteps. I'm sorry. I guess I should have told you—"

That night Sheila told Mark all about the *ghost* upstairs. At first he smirked skeptically at her, but Sheila found she had no problem accepting this amazing fact. Though she had never believed in such things, her heart calmed when she said the words aloud. She was okay with it, and, strangely, so was Joey.

"So the girl in the window and the noise upstairs—was a ghost?" Mark questioned looking from Joey to Sheila.

She nodded but Joey chimed in. "She's not a ghost, Dad. Yesterday she told me she'd be leaving—she said she was gonna keep my picture of her, take it with her. She told me to say goodbye to you, Momma."

That night the whole family slept soundly for the first time since they moved into the new apartment. In the following days, no one saw the upstairs curtains move and no little face appeared at the window. Sheila found solace from her mourning in mothering Joey.

A month after the family moved into their new home, Sheila walked out into the sunny afternoon to retrieve the mail. A cold feeling came over her as she saw the return address on an envelope. It was from the adoption agency. She pulled out a single sheet of paper.

Dear Mrs. Dillard,

It was a pleasure to meet you, even though it was under such sad circumstances. There is an additional bit of information I thought you might like to know. The last known address of Abby and her parents was: Mountain View Apartments, #1, Roy, Utah.

A small photo fell from the envelope and floated gently to the ground.

Sheila picked it up and a little girl with large brown eyes stared back at her. Dark chocolate curls framed her angelic face.

Echo City *was founded in 1854 as a stagecoach stop. In 1860 the Pony Express couriers came through, and build a station. In 1868 the Railroad came and the population increased. The 1929 depression was one of the reasons Echo became a ghost town.*

8. Echoes from the Past

Sherry Hogg

Beau

I guess he stopped shooting when he thought I was dead. Truth is, I'm pretty sure I'm done for too. Down and blasted to pieces, I feel the blood rushing out of me and into the ground and brush all around. My eyes are blinking slowly all on their own, and I can feel a bubbling rise in my throat, making its way slowly to the corners of my mouth.

Halfway up the hillside, I see Jeb stepping out from behind a rock pile and starting toward me. Jumping and sliding through red dirt and brush, he's whistling an old tune that reminds me of our mother.

Eyes squeezed tight, I see her, standing at the clothes line, barefoot, pulling worn sheets off to fold.

The late afternoon sun fills the billowing cotton up with a bright warming glow, and Mama's voice rises above it like a light breeze. *Oh Susanna, Oh don't you cry for me.* Sweet like a fragrance, the sound fills me up and I feel myself floating toward it.

Suddenly, the snuffling of my old bay, Blue, brings me back to the moment, my pain and predicament. I feel the velvety softness of his nose bumping at me gently, and I wish like hell I could grab a fistful of mane and leg up like I have a million times before. Instead, I lay motionless, waiting for my brother to get down off the mountain and tell me why he's gone and gut-shot me like some mangy low-down horse thief.

The moon fills up the sky above me, bright and full, and across its face pictures of my life come floating by, one after another, like an old set of tintypes. Lying there, waiting on Jeb, I realize there isn't an image without him in it. My brother is there in every picture, every frame, every moment of my life, and not one of them explains why he just filled me full of lead.

***

Our town was a small overland stage station that cropped up one day in the middle of nowhere—a board store, post office, saloon, and blacksmith shop. The Overland Mail superintendent built and ran them all so there wasn't much for anyone else to do but work for him or at the saw mill, or quarry, which is what my daddy did.

Mama had gone screaming and crying with the last baby, and was buried up by the school under a windy poplar, so it was just my brother and me raising each other up, trying our best to stay out of Daddy's way. He took Mama's going pretty hard and the saloon saw the best of him after that. It turned him out stumbling and undone most nights, and it was up to Jeb and me to get him in bed and out of his boots till morning. With the sun we had to roust him and get them on again so he could make the first whistle at the quarry. Watching him and old Sorrely ride away into the cedars was the best part of the day, signaling complete and utter freedom for Jeb and me, and being young boys in open country, we made the most of it.

Surrounded by a wilderness of red rock cliffs, canyons, and wide river valleys, Echo City was the ideal spot for a couple of young hooligans to grow and prosper. The Overland Stage route ran directly through town, providing a steady stream of characters pulling in on wagon trains, mail and passenger stages, and coming in from the coal and silver mines up in Chalk Creek and Park City. Our favorite pastime was hiding behind rock and brush, confounding and tormenting whatever came within range of our pea shooters, sling shots, and—eventually—our Winchesters. Raggedy jack rabbits dodging through the sage, night scavenging coyotes slipping between brush and rock, or sissified wagon travelers rolling out of Echo Canyon, dazed, worn and dirty, were all fair game.

When we'd grown, we took what work we could get, like running cattle or coal wagons, but mostly we just rode around free as the wind, wreaking havoc and avoiding authority. Seemed like somebody was always after us—Daddy, storekeepers, angry Mormons, the town constable. But Jeb and I stuck together come hell or high water and neither one of us had much use for anyone else in the world till Miss Fanny came along. That girl was something else altogether.

Jeb

Fanny seemed completely surprised when my hands closed around her throat and I dug my thumbs into her windpipe. She knew I loved her more than anything breathing, so it makes sense she wouldn't expect me to choke the life out of her. There was just no way around it. It was this or let her run off with some California cowboy, just flying through town. I loved her too much for that.

I told her so too, so there wouldn't be a misunderstanding. "I love you so much baby, you'll always be my girl," I murmured, squeezing tighter, and I watched the look in her eyes turn from disbelief to terror.

She was flopping around and flailing arms and legs right up to the last, but never took her dying eyes off mine. They were completely filled with unstoppable rage and murderous intent and I could tell that if I let her up now, I'd soon find myself with a Bowie knife in the back or in front, whichever she could get to first. I knew I had to finish it, though I would sorely miss her company.

When she was still, I laid myself down next to her and held her tiny frame close, running my hand over the curve of her hip and softly stroking her hair. In the struggle, a few golden strands had come loose and fallen over her cheek and eyes. I brushed them back and gazed adoringly into her fixed expression. Her eyes had glazed over without closing, which suited me just fine, 'cause I never did want her to stop looking at me. Exhausted and content, I relaxed into her cooling body and drifted off to sleep.

The room was dim when I woke, with the last slanting light of day making its way over the window pane and onto the bed. Fanny's eyes were on me still. I smiled. Noticing her right hand was clenched in a tiny little fist, I took it between my own, stroking the fingers to relax them, but she was not having it. The fist was set in stone. I left off, rolled over and put my mind to deciding what to do next.

With night coming, there would be plenty of time and cover to do what needed to be done, but it was more than a one-man operation. So I tucked Fanny in, pulling the bed covers up over her dress and shoulders, smoothed her hair, kissed her cheek, and headed downstairs to find my brother.

Beau

It had just gone dark outside and the saloon wasn't much lit—a couple of dingy oil lamps hanging over tables in the center of the room were all that stood between us and total darkness. At a table in the back corner, I was jawing with Old Dan, fellow reprobate and cattle rancher. Dan had been selling stock to the railroad since they hit Cheyenne. With the pony express office shutting down, the telegraph coming and the railroad too, there was a lot to go over.

"Mark my words, boy," Dan snarled, shaking a bony finger at the end of my nose, "that new saloon going up across the street is just the start. When them railroad people start showing up here, this place is gonna turn itself upside down. You won't be able to walk down the street without stepping into a whorehouse." I was about to tell him how much the idea appealed to me when I noticed Jeb on the staircase, coming down from the upstairs rooms. With more than his usual swagger he made his way over to the table and helped himself to a chair.

"Maudie, bring us another bottle—we're celebratin'!" He arched his eyebrows in my direction and flashed a toothy grin. It was a little too toothy and his eyes had something wild in them that made me uneasy. Old Dan too, 'cause he stood up right away, made his excuses, and backed out the door. Maudie brought over a bottle of tangleleg. Jeb cracked it open and poured us each a snort.

"So what's the occasion, brother?" I asked, though the look in his eye made me pretty sure I didn't want to know. I'd seen that look many times before. Jeb had a sadistic streak a mile long. More than once he'd had me come running to see something he'd done and was over the moon excited about. Most often it would turn out to be something that used to be alive but wasn't, all splayed out or skinned or broken to pieces. It made me queasy and I didn't see it going anywhere good, but there was never any stopping Jeb or even talking to him, so I let it be.

"Well, little Beau, there just ain't no way for you to know what the occasion is without you follow me up them stairs and see for yourself." Jeb stood, pushing back his chair and grabbing the bottle off the table. As I followed him reluctantly, a mighty dread began to rise and swirl in the pit of my stomach. At the top of the stairs, Jeb turned left and came to a stop in front of the third door, painted blue and marked with the number seven.

I'd been in and out of these rooms a few times, and I knew right well who this one belonged to— Fanny Mae, the little piece of sweetness who'd showed up last fall, having hitched a ride with a Mormon drover all the way from Fort Kearney. She hadn't planned on getting off in Echo City, but it seems Brother Olson had made up his mind before they left the Platte that this golden-haired beauty was destined to be lucky wife number seven. Fanny had other plans and jumped the wagon while her intended was stocking up on whiskey at the Echo Saloon. She slipped in the back at Maudie's and threw herself on the old madame's mercy. Maudie knew a sure thing when she saw it and took her right in, billing Fanny as the blond-haired, blue-eyed maiden of the west. The girl was a natural and within a week had more business than she could handle.

Of all the rowdy cowboys busting down Miss Fanny's door, my brother was the most ardent, the most insistent, the most difficult to turn away. He was taken over by the girl, and from the first day he set eyes on her, thought of little else. I would have counseled him severely on the foolish and fruitless nature of falling in love with a whore, but I knew Jeb, and there was no point in it.

As he opened the door to her room, the dread I had swirling around in my gut took a turn to straight horror. From the doorway I could see little Fanny was dead and gone. The wide open, bulging eyes proved the ghastly point that she had not gone willingly or in peace. Struck dumb with disbelief, I looked to my brother standing triumphantly at the bedside. The oversize grin was pasted all over his face and my brain scrambled to make sense of the horrific scene.

Jeb spoke first, "Well, whaddya think, brother Beau? I've got her now, don't I?" I closed the door and crossed the floor to where Jeb was standing, trying not to look at the bed and its occupant. Grabbing the bottle, I tipped it back and downed about a third. Steadied, I turned to my lunatic brother and demanded, "What the hell happened here?"

Without hesitating, Jeb launched into a story that involved him dropping by to see Fanny, finding her writing a love letter to a boy who came through with the Pony Express, confronting her, and being told in no uncertain terms that she loved the boy, planned on going to California with him, that he was coming through to pick her up in two weeks, and that was that.

"But she ain't going now, is she?" he finished triumphantly. "Guess Miss Fanny ain't going nowhere without me from now on."

I'd never seen my brother so pleased with himself, and a combination of loyalty to him and fear of his insanity made me ignore the heinous nature of the crime and focus instead on cleaning it up. We rolled Fanny up in her sheet and waited for the saloon to close. Taking a shovel from the back stoop, we carried the girl across the dark street and buried her under the new saloon. The partly constructed building gave easy access to everything underneath, and we hollowed out a shallow grave under the foundation.

We took turns digging and no one spoke. While I dug, Jeb spent his time rubbing and stroking Fanny's little fist. He was determined to pry it open, to relax the fingers, to soften and spread them out— and he tried to close her eyes. But Fanny seemed determined to have her way in this if nothing else. When the digging was done, we left her there in her sheet, eyes bulging, fist clenched, covered in a thin layer of dirt and lye.

Jeb

I don't think I'd have killed Fanny if I'd known she wouldn't stay dead. The very morning after we buried her, she rose right up and started following me around like the vindictive demon that she was. I took it as a sign of her stubbornness. Even Jesus waited three days.

And stubborn she was. I couldn't go anywhere without her. Waking up in the morning, I felt Fanny next to me in the bed, cold and vaporous, chilling my bones and filling my heart with dread. During the day she followed me around from store to saloon and out on the trail. Riding the canyon, I could feel her ahead of and behind me, and looking down on me from the rocky cliffs above. Empty bushes rattled as we passed, and boulders came tumbling down from the mountainside with no warning. Soldier, my trusty old roan, got so jumpy he near threw me off a dozen times a ride. If I got off to take a piss I had to tether him hard to a tree or he'd bolt and run flat out, head down all the way back to town.

Hoping to appease Fanny, I took a job at Maudie's tending bar, and moved into her old room. I cut a hole in the plaster wall and made a shrine, stowing her letter and a 5 dollar gold piece she'd got from her lover. Still, she was ever present, moving the curtains in still air, sliding blankets to the floor as I slept. Her voice and her thoughts filled my head with her need, insisting and urgent. I knew Fanny wanted something from me, and one chilly autumn night, she stood illuminated in the moonlit window of our room and told me what it was.

Beams of moonlight moved and shifted through the thin cotton of her dress and translucent skin. Mesmerized by her, as I had always been, I immediately agreed to do her bidding.

Fanny wanted her cowboy, and being as I had deprived her of him by choking the life out of her, it was my job to fetch and deliver him. I set myself to it. We caught him at the mouth of Echo Canyon coming in full speed ahead on his pony, bags full of mail and messages. Beau and I had set up a trip line, and his horse hit it flying. The boy launched skyward, while the pony rolled, and tumbled through the brush, bleeding out and nearly decapitated. When the cowboy hit the ground, he was broken to pieces, but I stepped right up and put a bullet between his eyes—his suffering ended there. We buried him just before sun up, next to my Fanny, and I went home and to bed, to savor a bit of well-earned peace and quiet.

Beau

My very last breaths are rattling my bones, when Jeb finally makes it down the hill and to my body. He pokes me a couple of times in the ribs with the barrel of his Winchester.

"Not dead yet, son? Want me to take care of that for you?" He waits for a reply I have no way of making. He kneels down next to me, and puts a hand on my forehead, as if to fix things. "Look, if you must know, I'm sorry. I really am, but you know Miss Fanny. The girl wants what she wants and there's no talking to her out of nothing.'"

I have no idea what he's talking about and it must show in my face, 'cause he keeps on.

"That was her you danced with tonight at Maudie's. Didn't you know? She wore a boa? That was Fanny. And she wants you, so here you go."

He pulls the .45 out of his holster and plugs me between the eyes.

Jeb

I'm not sure how many men we killed, Beau and me, trying to keep that woman happy. Half a dozen or so—I lose count. And killing them wasn't the worst of it. Dragging the dead weight of their carcasses through the basement window of the new saloon, across the floor, and down my secret trap door and tunnel to Fanny's lair usually wore me clean out. It was a body a year for three or four years and then it was Beau himself she wanted.

She told me like she always did—came down from the room with a mask and a red feather boa and danced with the boy...a waltz. When she wrapped the boa around his neck, I knew he was the one she wanted and I got it taken care of. Now they're all laid out there in a row under the floorboards of the new saloon, Fanny and all her boys, Beau included.

Come spring I've decided I'll be joining them. I have a little bottle of strychnine I'll be mixing with some good rye whiskey and laying myself down for a nap under the new saloon. I'm tired as hell, I really am. I could use a good rest, and I'd sure like to see my old brother, Beau.

The Wasatch Back *is part of the Rocky Mountains in Utah. It includes cities such as Park City, Morgan, and Heber City and is home to numerous ski resorts. It is located on the eastern side of the Wasatch Range.*

9. The Lost Mines

Brenda Hattingh

May 27th
11:30 am

*D*ear Journal, Kevin and I have decided to start documenting our adventures! He says every day with me is an adventure, so I had better do the writing, because he would never stop writing. Sweet or lazy? Haha. I'm choosing to go with sweet. He's sitting next to me in the car right now, driving slower than my grandmother as per usual. I should have driven, but then who would write? We're headed up to the silver mines of Park City!!! We'll see if we can even get in. Apparently they've been closed off, but we have our ways...

We're going to see the mines for ourselves and maybe even run into some ghosts! Oooooooh, spooky! According to the Internet, among other things, we may or may not run into down there are: the woman who rides her horse through the tunnels at 200 ft below surface level, the man in the yellow slicker who shows up before a deadly accident, and random miners looking for missing body parts! Apparently the lower rungs of ladders have also disappeared, preventing people from getting out of the mines, haha. We even joked about bringing some extra rungs just in case.

These are the things we brought with us to aid in the adventure: Two flash lights, extra batteries, a metal, extendable ladder, granola bars and water. Oh, and my watch. Kevin gave it to me before we went on our Grand Canyon adventure. It's waterproof and shatterproof and lights up in the dark. I need it for my diary entries. Lol.

We'll check in with you again later! Ciao for now!

2:21 pm

Dear Journal, holy crap, we're in!!!

Goooooooood grief, that was scary! We found an opening that had been boarded up and had a big "No Trespassing" sign nailed over it, but the wood was pretty much decayed and it was easy pulling all of it apart. We managed to get the ladder down inside and there was barely enough space to get my butt through the hole to climb down the rickety ladder! Must lay off those big brunches ☺ Honestly, that was kinda scary, but we did it! It's dark down here, like dark *dark. You seriously can't see your hand in front of your face. Glad we have the flash-lights! So far no miners with missing limbs and no fair-haired maidens on horseback. Our ladder still has all its rungs and there are no yellow slickers in sight, haha. We're going to explore! Ciao for now!*

5:00 pm

Dear Journal, this place is awesome! We've been down so many different tunnels. It's a maze down here! Kevin calls it Amaze-ing ☺. And we haven't gotten lost yet, lol. We keep going back to the entrance to make sure we know where we're at. I feel like we should have brought bread crumbs, but Kevin says that they may have attracted some hungry, limbless miners. I have a pretty good sense of direction, so I think we'll be fine.

5:25 pm

Dear Journal, Kevin is getting a little annoyed at my constant journal entries, but I want us to be able to look back at our adventures and remember every exciting moment. I wish I had kept a journal when we went on our epic three-day hike in the Grand Canyon. You just don't remember everything after a while. Anyway, I just wanted to write about how sweet Kevin is. I've offered to carry the backpack with our supplies several times, but he refuses to let me. What a gentleman.

5:45 pm

Dear Journal, Right now we're sitting down and having some granola bars and water, how romantic. Kevin pulled a blanket out of the backpack and laid it down for us! That's pretty sweet. I'm always surprised when he thinks of something sweet like that, lol.

5:55 pm

Dear Journal, OMG OMG OMG! Kevin just proposed!!! I can't believe it! I love him so much! The ring is beautiful, and it's made with Park City Silver! It has a sapphire instead of a diamond! I told him never to get me a diamond with all the bloodshed they've caused. And look at that! He listens after all! Holy hell, I'm in heaven! (Even though I'm technically underground) I really wish we hadn't left our phones in the car so that I could take a pic right now! I told him I had to stop and write about it, but I think we might seal the deal down here. I mean how many people can say they've done it in the silver mines of Park City!? I just hope there are no creepy crawlies down here, eek! I guess THAT'S why he brought the blanket.

6:23 pm

Dear Journal, I'm so embarrassed! I was down to my underwear and some guy showed up out of nowhere and yelled for us to "GET THE HELL OUT OF HERE!" It was kind of creepy. I think he was standing there looking at us over Kevin's shoulder for a while before I noticed him. And when he yelled at us, Kevin jerked his head and hit my teeth with his teeth really hard, ouch! I'm so happy though, I don't even care! But I feel I do have to mention (cue the Twilight Zone *music . . .), the guy was wearing a yellow slicker!!! I guess they have people patrol the mines to keep people like us out, which makes it feel a little less scary and daring ☺ But I think we have the best engagement story of all time! And the yellow slicker is definitely a nice touch.*

6:42 pm

Dear Journal, Someone is messing with us. The bottom rungs of our ladder are gone.

7:32 pm

Dear Journal, we tried to pull ourselves up by the rungs that are still there. It's a lot more difficult than you may think. Then Kevin tried to boost me up, but my hand slipped off the rung and I fell. I think my ankle is sprained and my left wrist is killing me. Kevin got super frustrated and he lost it. I hate it when he gets mad like that. I mean why can't you look on the bright side? We're here together, we just got engaged and I'm right-handed, so I can still write. I used to work as a camp counselor for outdoor wilderness first aid camps and the first thing we learned was to keep calm. I'm also going to add "stay positive" to that, because a nega—

7:49 pm

Kevin ripped the journal out of my hand and threw it!

Him: I'm so sick of that stupid journal!

Me: What the hell, Kevin?

Him: Can't you see we're in trouble here?!

Me: We're fine! We're not dying!

Him: If we don't get out of here, we will!

So I started crying and he felt really bad and put his arms around me, which was sweet. I hate it when we fight, but he's always so good at apologizing and making me feel better ☺ We talked about what we should do and then we heard something in the tunnel. It sounded like someone running. We think it's the guy that told us to get out of here. Kevin said he's going to look, which freaks me out, because I don't think it's a good idea for us to separate, but I can't exactly hobble after him on my bum ankle and he didn't want to lose track of the guy in case he knows another way out.

8:14 pm

Dear Journal, Kevin isn't back yet and it's making me nervous. What if he got lost? What if he hurt himself? Oh no! I sound like my mother ☹ What if he's dead in a ditch? I'm being silly. He'll be back soon. Staying positive!

8:17 pm

Dear Journal, I'm going to look for Kevin.

8:42 pm

Dear Journal, I walked, or rather hobbled, down the tunnel that I saw Kevin go down, but I couldn't find him. I've called his name several times, but he's not answering. I know he could be close though. One time we were in the caves in Joshua Tree and we couldn't hear each other when we were in two different tunnels very close to one another.

8:56 pm

Dear Journal, I just realized that I should go back to the entrance. If he goes back there and doesn't find me, he might go looking for me again and we'll keep missing each other. Maybe I'll leave him a note saying "stay here" and then look for him again.

9:14 pm

I'm lost

9:37 pm

I just saw Kevin!!! He wouldn't answer me when I called his name! So weird! Maybe he didn't hear me? He had that look of being very intent on something, like when he's playing his video games and can't focus on anything else. He was going into a tunnel that split off in two different directions and I think I went down the wrong one to follow him. He's gotta be close. My ankle is killing me, but I'm staying positive.

2:30 am

Kevin is dead.

Don't want to write anymore but I want someone to know where to find him. At the bottom of a mine shaft. Don't know what to say. Sorry

3:43am

Don't want to get out. Don't know how to tell his parents. Don't want to live.

5:50am

I can't stop crying. But Kevin wouldn't give up. Going to find the way out.

Going in circles. Keep ~~stopping~~ ending at the mine shaft. Flash light flickering. Batteries are in the backpack. O God! It's in Kevin's backpack. On his back. I have to get it. Don't wanna write anymore,

~~but if I don't get out~~ but want family to know what happened.

Think my leg is broken. Tried to climb down mine shaft for batteries. ~~I fell on Kevin~~ I have the batteries. Not sure I can get out. So much pain. Perhaps they'll find our car and come and get us. But we hid it so well. So stupid.

Mom... Dad... I'm sorry... I love you . . .

Tried to climb out. Not enough energy. Too much pain.

Trying to be quiet, not to cry. Don't want to wake Kevin, but I'm scared... and it hurts!

Can't feel my leg. Why are there worms in his hair? I pulled them out. His face is blue. Maybe he's cold.

6:12 am or pm?

Fell asleep. Woke up with my head on Kevin's chest. His chest isn't moving. His skin is so cold. Tried to put his arm around me but it's too stiff. His eyes are open, looking at me. I wish he would say something. This place is too quiet. Silence hurts.

I love you I love you I love you I love you I love you I love you I love you I love you I love you I love you I love you I love you I love you I love you I lo.....

Kevin's eyes won't stop looking. Tried to close them, but it won't...

So... dark...

The Broad's Fork, Twin Peaks, *at 11,330 feet, towers over the Salt Lake Valley and Utah's capital—Salt Lake City. It is part of the Wasatch Front in Utah. SLC is named after the Great Salt Lake. It is nicknamed 'Crossroads of the West' after the first transcontinental railroad and two major cross-country freeways—I-15 and I-80—which intersects in the city. SLC is also known for its ski resorts and hosted the 2002 Winter Olympics. It is the industrial banking center of the United States.*

10. The Unknown

Dimitria Van Leeuwan

I stood in the dusk of a gray January day, looking up at the building that housed the Fort Douglas Museum. I hadn't even known it was here before I got this assignment from my history professor at the University of Utah. The building was low and wide, wedged sideways into the hillside with a veranda running across the entire front. It sat at the base of the towering mountains, overlooking the Salt Lake Valley. It was pretty old, built over a hundred years ago, if I remembered right.

I sighed, and trudged through crusty snow up to the steps, when out of nowhere in the dim light, the alien white face of a barn owl swooped over my head in a slow, buoyant flight. As it passed, heading north, it let out a piercingly loud, rasping scream that echoed in the quiet street.

In my tribe, the Navajo, to see an owl is not a good sign. Back home on the reservation I learned that if an owl is flying north it's really bad. It's like a warning. An owl is a message that could be about death.

It made my hands shake; I guess it scared me pretty bad. I was stopped in my tracks in the street. Finally I took a deep breath and went up the stairs and tried to open the door. It stuck a little and I hurt my hand when I forced it open.

Once inside, it was warm and dusty, and the first thing I saw was a staged scene with mannequins dressed as soldiers, warming their hands over an artificially lit fire. I signed the guestbook, and was greeted by Su; a middle-aged woman with no-fuss short hair and an intelligent face. I was still a little shaken up but I tried to hide it. "I'm Danielle," I introduced myself, and told her I was there to do research on the early days of the Fort.

She told me I could start by looking around, and to just ask if I had any questions. I wandered through the door to the right of the entrance, into a long room filled with objects and memorabilia from the long history of the fort. At the far end of the room was a giant mural depicting white soldiers bracing themselves behind a large wooden board, shooting at a group of Indians who were returning fire, huddled behind a grassy bank.

I was looking at it when I felt something like cold breath on the back of my neck. I raised my shoulders to shrug it off, and glanced around the room. There were a handful of people there, a family with a couple of teenage boys, but no one near me. No one else seemed uncomfortable.

I spent more time looking through the place, at the murals and photographs, at the many weapons, cooking utensils, even musical instruments that were left over from the almost century and a half of activity at Fort Douglas.

After a while I went to find Su, and asked her if she had any books or documents with information about the fort in the 1800's.

"We're about to close up, but you're welcome to look through the library for a few minutes," she told me, and led me to a room in the back.

There was an exhibit room with one wall of books, and through that room another, smaller one that wasn't open to the public. It was a small rectangle, with books along all four walls, and shelves crammed with books and magazines took up the majority of space in the middle of the room, leaving a person-sized walkway around it. Su pointed me in the direction of what I was looking for and left me to browse.

On the first shelf I found a dark green book with gold writing that said: "Fort Douglas, Utah, A Frontier Fort, 1862 – 1991, by Charles G. Hibbard."

I opened it and began to read the preface. It said: "Fort Douglas was established in 1862 for the purpose of protecting the Overland Mail Route and telegraph lines from depredations by hostile Indians."

I lowered the book for a moment and took a deep breath. This was going to be a little weird.

I knew that in later years, WWII, Navajos were important assets to the United States war effort, and "code talkers" were extremely valuable in keeping information about our troops safe; but in the early days the main purpose of Fort Douglas, when it was still *Camp* Douglas, was to keep my people away from the settlers. The United States was at war with the Indians.

"Oh!" I jumped, realizing someone was standing behind me. I turned to see who it was but the small room was empty. I felt a surge of unexplainable fear. I decided it was a good time for me to leave.

I walked around the shelves to get to the door and found myself staring at a stocky man in a dirty blue uniform, with very dark brown hair and a full beard. His eyes widened in shock, or maybe anger, and he quickly turned toward the wall and disappeared before my eyes.

I stared at the doorway, too scared to move, but the sight of Su coming around the corner made me jump and let out a little scream.

"I..." I just pointed at the wall. "I just saw someone! He just vanished!"

She looked at the place where I was pointing and after a moment, she said philosophically,

"Well, I guess you've met Clem. Did he look like a soldier?"

I nodded, "I think so."

"Did he say anything?

I shook my head.

"I've heard his footsteps before, but I myself have never seen him," she said pleasantly. "I guess you're one of the lucky ones."

"Clem?" I asked her.

"Well, that's the name a group of boy scouts gave him when they heard about our resident ghost. No one is really sure who he is, but plenty of people have heard or seen him," she said all this matter of factly. "I came to tell you we're closing up now."

She waited until I walked out past her, and I couldn't help looking back as I left, goose bumps on my arms. Su was still looking at the spot I'd pointed out.

On the short drive back to my apartment I was really freaked out and kept on checking my back seat. Of course every time I turned around it was empty.

***

Over the next week, I spent some time reading the books I'd taken home with me, and did a lot of online research, even looking up people who had died at the Fort. I was really at this point going beyond what I needed for my history class. I was just super interested, and kind of hooked. I planned to go back to the Museum for more information. I was still a little scared at the thought of it, but really a little curious too.

The next day I drove toward the Fort thinking about all the many different people who had lived and died there. On a whim, I drove first to the nearby Fort Douglas cemetery. It was a gray, windy day, with patches of snow left here and there on the ground. I started at the east end of the large square of land, picking my way carefully over uneven ground, reading the white headstones as I went. I stopped in front of a row of old headstones that read *Unknown*.

A cold wind started up, whipping my hair around my face. I felt a deep chill, like there were spirits in the air around me. No one was there but again I felt like I wasn't alone. I thought immediately of the man in the back library, and I thought about the owl.

At the Fort I sat down with Su in her office. Her desk overflowed with papers and books.

"I have some questions," I said. "I read that soldiers in the 1860's endured tough situations—terrible weather, long walks, and no retirement. Why would anyone volunteer to be a soldier in those conditions?" I asked.

She immediately said, "Because they had nothing to lose. These were people that often had no land or families, no other jobs to support themselves with."

I nodded. "I guess that is understandable."

Then I remembered the peculiar headstones in the cemetery. "I saw that some of the headstones say 'Unknown'. Why? How would something like that happen?"

Su leaned back and pointed at a painting on the wall behind her desk. "That situation right there is one example."

It was of a soldier held captive, surrounded by Indians on horseback.

"You'll notice his jacket has been thrown onto the ground." Su said. "If they kill him, it may be months, or years before his body is found. There might be nothing there to identify him."

I stared at the painting, looking at the men on horseback, wondering how they felt. Then I looked at the prisoner, his arms pinned behind his back, and I thought about the soldiers I'd read about, the ones who had nothing to lose. As I thought about him, I felt suddenly cold, and my head swam. I heard, as if from far away, men shouting. I saw their angry faces.

I looked back at Su, "Soldiers do what they do because they think it is the right thing, don't they? On both sides of the battle..."

Su smiled wisely, and then lifted one pile of papers, then a few more, until eventually she found what she was looking for: a large book with a blue linen cover. She passed it to me and I opened it to find a large portrait of a civil war era soldier. "These are some personal histories of soldiers from the 1800's. You might find them interesting."

I thanked her, and took the book home with me that night but didn't immediately have a chance to read it. I talked with my roommate Sidra later, after dinner. I had told her all about the Fort and what happened to me there.

"I still can't really wrap my brain around the vanishing man. It was really weird, but I swear I really saw him!"

She smiled at me, a gentle, sympathizing smile. "It's pretty intense the first time something like that happens, huh? Like, you *know* something just happened, but it *couldn't* have. She tucked a short curl of her dyed black hair behind her ear and tilted her head.

Sidra was a modern dance major at the U, and was very in touch with her feelings. "It was probably a spirit of someone who used to be stationed at the Fort," she continued. "Maybe it's bored."

I didn't like all this talk of spirits. My family doesn't take that stuff lightly. "Yeah, maybe," I said.

I excused myself and went to my room where I opened the nightstand drawer by my bed and took out a small leather pouch. Gently, I opened it. Inside was a fine gold dust—corn pollen, or táádidíín, the Navajo word for it. It's sacred to us—a very important part of our rituals. I always felt good when I held the pouch and experienced its good energy. My mother had given it to me the last time I went home. I placed it in my purse so I could keep it nearby wherever I went now.

Then I decided to call my mom and tell her everything that had happened to me.

We talked for an hour, and afterward I felt a lot better. She told me maybe I better not go back there—to the Fort. But she assured me everything would be fine, and they would have a ceremony for me when I came home for my next visit.

These ceremonies were always such an amazing, feel-good experience; to have my family and people close to me, sit with me all night, working through what was bothering me and giving me hope and peace and strength. As the sun came up, after the ceremony, I would go outside and be welcomed by the beautiful soft light at dawn with birds singing.

Thoughts of those peaceful mornings made me decide to put all of what happened behind me. But then my eyes went to the book Su had loaned me.

I opened it on the table in front of me, carefully turning each page. I looked over each face, lined from hardship and exposure; read some of their stories, their letters, newspaper articles that had been compiled to go along with their photos. I looked into their eyes, hoping to find something that would tell me what kind of persons they were, what were their lives like?

It was getting late, my eyes were tired, but I couldn't stop looking. I couldn't put the book away. Toward the back of, I turned a page and my heart missed a beat. It was an old photo, stained and faded, but unmistakable—it was the bearded man I had seen in the doorway! I stared at it, and read the caption: *John Clements, 1863.* I looked at his dark eyes, which in this photo were crinkled at the corners with laugh lines. Despite the full beard he looked young, and strangely innocent. Not the angry and distraught face that I had seen in the library. *What had happened to him to change him so much? What had he seen? What had he done?*

I read the short notification with the photo.
Born: Minnesota, 1840
Reported missing while on patrol duty

I had to go back to the museum one last time not only to return the book but also to... I don't know... get some kind of closure? I know his name now. I won't be able to prove it to anyone and he might be buried in one of those unknown graves... we'd never know. I felt a kind of sadness, but at the same time an understanding, for all those people who lived over a century ago, who lived with courage during difficult times—who fought with passion, maybe blinded to the bigger picture, not knowing that all too soon there would be an even bigger war—a war in which they'd all fight on the same side.

Back at the museum, I went straight to the room with the mural. I waited and when there were no more visitors I said aloud: "John, I just want you to know, there's no hard feelings..." I swallowed at the sudden sadness that caused a lump in my throat.

I turned, seeing something out of the corner of my eye, and like a fleeting shadow I saw *him*. But something was different this time. His eyes were sorrowful. He raised them and looked right at me, his expression changing to one of wonder.

Once again he faded, but not before I saw a hint of a smile light up his eyes.

Mount Timpanogos, *at 11,752 feet, towers over the Utah Valley, which includes cities such as Lehi and Provo. It is the second highest mountain in the Wasatch Range. Heavy winter snowfall is common and avalanche activity is high in winter and spring. It is home to Timpanogos Cave National Monument. The word Timpanogos comes from the Timpanogos tribe who lived in the surrounding valleys from AD 1400. The name translates as "rock" (tumpi-), and "water mouth" or "canyon" (panogos).*

II. Rayne Dance

Lynda West Scott

Oh, Rayne," I heard my sister, Evie say. Her voice sounded choked with emotion. I turned and saw tears trickling down her cheeks.

"Evie! What's wrong?" I said, hurrying back to where she stood on the trail. I put my arms around her. "Are you okay?"

Her crying subsided, but I could feel a residual wet spot on my shoulder, where her head still rested. Real tears from my usually stoic sister flooded my mind with fear over things she might be hiding from me: Does she have cancer? Did her husband cheat on her? Did she lose her job? The unknown frightened me and I grabbed her hands and forced her to look at me.

"What's wrong?" I asked again, wondering if I really wanted to know.

"Do you think it's true?"

"Do I think what's true?" I tried to sound patient. "What are you talking about?"

"You know—Timpanogos. Do you really think the native people sacrificed her—the princess?"

The look on my face betrayed me and Evie lowered her head and blushed.

"It's just so sad. While we've been climbing the trail I couldn't get the thought out of my mind, of her jumping from the top of THIS Mountain to appease their god. To kill herself for rain..." She looked at me with wide eyes and sniffled. "Oh Rayne! What if you lived then, you'd be the sacrifice?"

"Why? Just because my name is . . ." And then her meaning hit me. *Rayne* in exchange for *rain* for the tribe!

For the millionth time I cursed my mother for giving me this ridiculous name. I know Mom meant to name me LaRayne, after some distant relative, but somehow she forgot the "La" part on the birth certificate and decided to just call me Rayne. I think she's regretted it as much as I have because our relationship has always been a bit contentious—like I'm the dark, rainy cloud in her life.

"I'm sorry," Evie said. The look on her face expressed far more than her words and I put my arms around her again.

"It's all right, but what's up with you? You never cry."

"I don't know," she said, sagging and looking confused.

I guided us to a nearby bench and watched a delightful waterfall close to the trail while we talked.

"For some reason this place is making me jumpy," Evie said. "Maybe reading about the legends in the Timpanogos National Park brochure set me off. I mean, even with a dozen different versions, the love affair of the beautiful princess Utahna or whatever her name was, and Red Eagle is so tragic."

I laughed awkwardly, thinking about the version that felt most real to me, the one where Utahna picked the black pebble from the bowl and became the one to be a sacrifice for her tribe. While she made the climb to jump off the mountain, Red Eagle saw her and became infatuated with her beauty. He convinced her he was the god Timpanogos and told her that being his wife would complete the sacrifice. He lived with her in the cave until she realized he had tricked her and she decided to fulfill her duty. Red Eagle found her body and carried her back to the cave, where he died next to her. Then the god Timpanogos felt sorry for the loss of their perfect love and created the great heart in the cave over them.

That cave is where Evie and I are headed because of some crazy impulse I had to see the place—like some irrational urge to re-visit something... but what?

I shrugged off my eccentricity and agreed with Evie; these stories were sad—but they were *legends*! Not truth. Evie had gone over the top with this. I felt like I had an alien creature sat next to me—and in a way I was right. Something had replaced my sister with a person I didn't know, or like. It didn't occur to me that maybe I was the one who'd been replaced. I stupidly thought Evie suffered from heat stroke that affected her thinking; perhaps the altitude played tricks with her mind.

"Maybe we should head down and try this another day," I said patting her on the back.

"You think I'm crazy, don't you?" She smiled and the warmth of it let me know the real Evie still lived.

"Well, you have to admit this is very unlike you. Honestly, I'm fine with putting this off. You didn't want to come anyway, and if I never see it, I'll live. Also, you know how claustrophobic I am. I could get in there and become the crazy one—what was I thinking!" I laughed and she joined me.

"No, this has been on your bucket list. I don't know why, because it cost a bunch of money to get here from California. But let's get it over with. We're over half way there and we've already paid for the tickets."

"I'll make a deal with you," I said. "If we get to the top and people are there who want our tickets, we'll just walk back down and enjoy the beautiful wildflowers." Secretly, I figured this would get us out of it, which was what I wanted at this point. It seemed likely because we saw a lot of people trying to get tickets, and since only sixteen people are allowed at a time, and the wait list was long, some of them might have decided to make the climb, enjoy the view and come back another day.

"Deal," Evie said.

I wondered if she felt the same way and decided, like me, to leave it to fate.

We got up from the bench by the waterfall and after a strenuous one and a half-mile walk to the cave entrance, at 6,730 feet above sea level, we low-landers were exhausted. I found myself wondering again why this had been on my bucket list to begin with, and why had it become so urgent for me in just the last month? Yes, this part of the country is beautiful and we'd had a wonderful trip, but I'm not a cave person, never have been. My heart beat faster. To my disappointment, no one at the top needed tickets and I resigned myself to a 55-minute tour of the cave that would fulfill whatever crazy whim of destiny had propelled me to this place.

Evie seemed delighted once we found ourselves inside. Meanwhile, I tried to block out everything so as not to panic over being thousands of feet below solid rock, where I could be crushed at any second. Words like frostwork, stalactites, stalagmites, and cave bacon, dashed through my head as I looked at the rock formations all around us, but I reeled when we reached The Great Heart.

So this was the formation representing the hearts of Utahna and Red Eagle! I stared at the huge stalactite and heard the tour guide state it was 5 feet 6 inches in length (my height) and weighed 4,000 pounds. It appeared translucent when the ranger shone a light on it.

At the sight of the luminous creation I forgot to breathe, and the cool 45 degree cave temperature chilled me to the bone. The rhythmic beat of this heart of stone pounded in my ears and pulsated through my whole being. *Am I going crazy?* I looked toward my sister, but she and the rest of our group seemed oblivious to me; their eyes locked on the guide.

I honestly don't know what happened next; I must have raced out of the cave. Outside in the sun, I squinted in the brilliant contrast to the dark cavern. My heart throbbed in my chest, mimicking the pace of the cold stone I'd left behind. My breathing became ragged as I charged up a hillside. Brambles tore at my arms and legs, yet still I ran, as if driven. I found myself on the western slope of Mount Timpanogos, zig-zagging steeply uphill until I reached a slot where two rock walls hemmed in the trail. I paused there for a second, trying to catch my breath, before I hurried on again. I had to reach the top. I had to make this climb, but why? All logic seemed to have left me as I tried to reason with myself. I felt driven in a way I had never experienced before and as I ran, I wondered if this was the same path Utahna had taken.

When I stopped next, about midway on the mountain, I saw the summit above me. Its raw splendor amazed me. Before I realized my feet were moving again, I found myself at the mountain's pinnacle, looking down at a large valley below, with a lake in the distance.

That's Utah Valley and Utah Lake, I reasoned, *but where are the houses? The freeways?* Then I noticed a small village with blue smoke rising out of tepee tops and a certainty struck me. This was Utah Valley in the 1400's, at the time Utahna lived. I glanced at the trail far below and saw the figure of a man—Red Eagle—waving to me. I somehow knew he wanted to stop my actions, but commitment to my cause—whatever that was—seemed vital to me.

Dread filled me as I realized some part of my crazy brain thought I was Utahna and I had been sent to appease the god Timpanogos. I slashed at my face and screamed, trying to wake myself from this hideous nightmare. *Why did I ever think of making this trip?* But, even as this question came to me, I knew, someone else made this decision for me. I never had a say in it.

"Wake up, wake up!" I screamed, but even as I did, my traitorous feet moved closer to the brink.

Maybe when I slip over the edge and begin to fall, I'll come to and find I've just fainted from my claustrophobic fear and I'm still in the cave with Evie.

I found myself hurtling through the air, down, down, down. I experienced everything—the feel of the wind rushing around me, the rocks coming closer, the sound of my screams trailing behind me—and only blackness when I landed on large boulders.

A voice echoed in my ears: *You are mine now, Rayne. You are my gift for saving your people, and you are my bride as Utahna could never be.*

Heber City is located in a breath-taking mountain valley in Utah. It has cool summers and abundant snowfall in winter. The Heber Valley Historic Railroad is located in Heber City. The Heber Creeper takes visitors on a nice slow-paced ride through the beautiful Heber Valley and Wasatch Mountains, around the extensive Deer Creek Reservoir, and alongside the cascading Provo River. Majestic Mount Timpanogos and Cascade Mountain, Sundance Ski Resort, the Tate Barn and Soldier Hollow can be seen from the train.

12. Blue Like the Water

Barbara Emanuelson

Keep her safe for me, Ellie," my Tom said as he adjusted his Air Force cap. His eyes filled with tears as he watched our little Mae at play with her dolly. Walking over to her, he planted a kiss on her golden curls.

"You know I will, Tommy," I assured him as he reached for me and pulled me close. He kissed my forehead and I rested my head on his chest. I don't know how long we stood like that in the small living room of our home near the Provo River. The only sound I heard was his heartbeat. Then a car honked outside.

Tales from The Wasatch and Beyond...

"Guess this is it," Tom said as he walked to the door. "Be good for your mama, Mae," he called, blowing a kiss to our daughter. "You'll be four soon. That means you're a big girl. Help your mama out, you hear?"

"Yes, Daddy," Mae answered, and then returned to combing her doll's hair.

"Don't forget, love," Tom said as he squeezed my shoulder.

I put my fingers on his lips. "I'll keep her safe."

"And yourself, too," he said, opening the door. He left quickly, not turning at first. Then he whipped his head around, just before he got into the Jeep. It was then that I saw the haunted expression in his eyes, as though he would memorize my face, this house, the pond out back, and the woods— everything that encompassed the life that we'd built. He mouthed the words *I love you,* and then he was gone.

I didn't wait to see him go down the dirt road, which was still dotted with remnants of late March snow. I simply went inside and turned to our child whose hair and eyes were just like my Tom's. She hummed and combed her dolly's hair. I found myself smiling, even as the tears spilled down my face. I tied my long auburn hair back and filled the sink with the breakfast dishes, making a mental tally of the housework I had to do that day, happy to have something that would keep my mind occupied. And so, I threw myself into keeping our home and raising our little girl.

The days turned into weeks, and weeks turned into months. I got an occasional letter from Tom, telling me of his fellow airmen, the different foods, where he was—even that he'd gotten a souvenir or two for Mae, a pair of earrings for me. He'd be bringing them home as soon as he could. I read his letters over and over.

I was glad for diversions such as swimming in the pond with Mae. The pond—it was our own special place. Mae loved the water, especially the way it tickled her little nose when she tried to swim. I'd hold her and we'd spin, making waves.

From time to time, we'd talk to the occasional passerby who happened upon this well-hidden bit of heaven on earth. And every morning I'd hear the sound of the Creeper as she whistled her way up the Cascade Mountains on her way to Provo. I was glad when they put in a train stop about a quarter-mile from our house. I could now easily get in and out when the heavy snows came. I could also get up the mountain for food and a bit of company, for I was hungry for more than the woods and the water, beautiful though they were. I could talk to people; see the shops in Heber City. And it would be easy to post my letters, even in winter.

From our house I could see the train as she chugged up the mountain. Sometimes it was a passenger train and other times only the engine. The conductor saw me one day as Mae waded in the late summer waters. He blew the horn. Soon, I waited for him—even as the green of summer became an autumn blanket of color mixed with the evergreens on the mountain. Every time the Creeper passed the conductor blew the unmistakable two long toots and I waved. The train and conductor became my good friends, something to look forward to. I did not feel so cut off and alone anymore. I even wrote to Tom about them.

I wrote Tom as often as I could. I'd drive our Oldsmobile Brougham up the mountain road to post them and eagerly open Tom's letters when they came. I read them over and over. They always ended the same, "Keep our Mae safe."

It was a warm Indian summer day when Tom's last letter came, though I didn't know it then. He wrote of the horrors in a war-torn part of the world, that he'd bombed another enemy plane. He's now known as "Eagle-eye." I could tell he liked the title. And he was excited. His tour of duty was nearly over. He might be home for Christmas. "Two more months, Ellie—hold on to that, darling. Tell Mae her Daddy will be home soon."

The week before Thanksgiving it snowed. There was no way into my little piece of land, except for the Creeper. Thank God I had plenty of food and things to occupy my time. I had bought a bolt of blue wool and lots of thread and even some lace for trim, and buttons that looked like pearly white drops. I planned to make matching clothes for Mae and me.

"Mama, could Sally have a dress too?" Mae asked.

"You bet she can, baby. Your dolly looks just like you already, blue eyes and all."

"Blue like the water, Mommy?"

"Yep! Blue like the water, my angel."

Before long, all three dresses were made, with long sleeves, lace trimmings, and white buttons at the cuffs and down the front. Proud of my accomplishment, I suggested we try our dresses on. We stood gazing in the mirror, Mae and I. She held her Sally close to her.

"Oh, look how pretty we are, Mama! We look like the pond!"

I laughed lightly as I snuggled with her. But a sudden chill came over me. The skin on the back of my neck prickled. I grabbed Mae by the shoulders and turned her around. I went down on my knees, facing her. "Don't ever go near the pond without me, Mae. You hear?"

"I won't Mama. But Sally loves to swim in the water with me."

"Sally doesn't like the pond in winter, Mae. She can't swim when it's cold outside."

"Okay, Mommy. We'll just walk there."

"*With Mommy*, Mae—never alone."

"All right, Mommy, never alone."

Mae went back to playing and she sang, "Blue like the water is the pretty dress I wear," to the Itsy Bitsy Spider melody.

As suddenly as the fear came, it was gone, and I breathed a silent prayer.

It was now the day before Thanksgiving. I took a chicken from the icebox. I was going to stuff it. I had made us a pumpkin pie, and I had some canned green beans and freshly baked rolls too. It would be a good supper tomorrow—even though it would be incomplete without Tom. But I was determined to have a holiday, despite the fact that I hadn't heard from him in weeks.

I called the War Department that morning, asking the man who answered the phone if there was any news about Tom.

"Ma'am, no news is probably good news. Go have a Happy Turkey Day. Something'll come up soon. It's real hard getting mail back and forth behind the lines. Try not to worry. I'm sure you'll get a letter soon."

He hung up. I sat down. Something wasn't right, and I knew it. But what could I do but pray? *Dear Lord, keep him safe,* I repeated over and over.

Thanksgiving came and went, and still no letter or word from Tom. I settled back into my normal routine as December came, complete with a fresh batch of snow late in the afternoon of the first day of the month. I went to bed that night, missing Tom as the cold wind blew its lonely song just outside the window in our bedroom.

I awoke early the next morning and dressed in the new blue dress, deciding that I should go to Mae's room to rouse her, so that we could see the new snow. We might build a snowman and share some hot cocoa and popcorn. My feet were cold as I stepped into my shoes. I thought it strange that the house should feel so chilled, even for a wintry morning like this for I knew that there was plenty of oil in the heater.

I walked across the small hall to Mae's room. She wasn't snug in her bed as I expected. Panicking,

I ran into the kitchen and then the living room, which was freezing cold. The wind whipped in through the open door, leaving a small snowdrift in the doorway. I ran around outside the house, not seeing my little Mae. Then I saw a shallow track almost covered by a new wave of snow—it led to the pond. Dread seized me, and my breaths came out as thick white puffs. I ran to the pond. On my way I slipped, not caring that I had made a mess of my blue dress, or that I was wet and freezing. Then I spotted Sally on top of the frozen pond. There appeared to be a darkened shallow patch right next to the doll.

"No... Oh, God, please, no!" I screamed. But even from where I was, I could see the shadow that lay just beneath the freshly frozen surface. I slipped and slid across the frozen pond, not caring that I might fall through. I fell to my knees near the shadow and banged at the thin ice with my fists. Finally there was a crack, and I threw myself on it, breaking through the ice, until I could seize my baby girl. I pulled her limp little form out of the icy water and onto my lap. I pressed her to my chest and rocked her to try and warm her frozen body.

I don't know how I got away from the pond—I only remember sitting in the snow, cradling her in my arms. My body felt numb, and yet there was so much pain that I ached from the inside out, impervious to my icy clothes and hair.

Then I heard mewling little sounds, tiny grunts that slowly made their way into wails and I realized it came from me. It was as though I had stepped out of my body now, watching this stranger holding and rocking a dead child, pressed close to her breast. And then I was back in my body, where the pain felt like shards of glass moving through my extremities and into my breaking heart. Suddenly it registered; this was my child—cold, frozen and blue. *Blue like the water...* Mae's words haunted me now.

"Mae... oh Mae," I cried over and over, covering my face with my trembling hands. "My baby... my baby... oh, dear God, my baby . . ."

Then the realization came and I whispered *"Tom, oh Tom, I failed to keep her safe. I did not take care of her the way a good mother should."*

"Why, oh why?" I demanded over and over, first of myself and then of God. "How could this have happened? Oh, God, how will I ever be able to forgive myself? Oh, Mae, how will you forgive your mama for sleeping so soundly? I didn't hear you leave. And how am I going to tell your Daddy, that our child is—dead?" Oh, sweet Jesus—I've failed him. Grief choked me.

If only... *if only!*

From a distance I heard the Creeper's horn blow... at first just the two toots, as usual, and then several more. I looked up—*my friends.* It was the engine only this time. As if in a dream I saw the train came to a halt; steam billowing into the freezing sky. From where I sat rocking my baby I saw the conductor struggling through the deep snow. He had a blanket with him, and without speaking he took my little Mae and wrapped her in it. He carried her to our house. He did not say much, just held my cold hand for a while and told me he would let the people in town know.

The funeral was very small. The conductor from the Creeper came, along with the shop owners of the store that I went to the most—that was all. The people from the ward wandered by afterward, a few at a time.

I hardly spoke to them but I heard them whisper.

"Still wearing that blue dress—"

"What a shame."

"She's sure her husband won't forgive her—"

"She keeps calling that doll 'Mae.'"

Yes, I wore the dirtied blue dress and held Sally close to me all the time. I could almost hear Mae sing, "Blue like the water, Mama?" And my own voice as the bitter words escaped my soul, "Blue like the water."

Tragedy struck once more the week after the funeral. Two men came to my house, one a clergyman and one an officer. They had a flag with them and Tom's flyer's cap. I can't forget the letter from the president, or the words the officer spoke as he handed them to me. "The people of the United States of America are grateful for your husband's bravery and service to the cause of freedom and democracy." He handed me the precious few things and saluted. Then they left.

Tom was buried next to Mae a week later, between the house and the pond. This time, even fewer came. They brought food and left. I was totally alone. All I had was an empty house, Tom and

Mae's clothes and—Mae's dolly. But I felt as though they were with me.

I'd go to their graves and cry. "Please forgive me," I begged over and over, sitting next to Tom's grave. To May I said, "I love you, sweetie. Mama loves her baby girl so very much."

It was early spring and a late March snow had left a new blanket, covering their graves. I sat in the stillness, the aching loneliness swept through me once again, harder and fiercer than it had since Tom's funeral. I rocked back and forth and hugged myself in my blue dress. I tried to will the hurt away, but it clung to me like the cold, wet snow that covered their graves. I stood up and looked at the pond. It wasn't frozen solid yet. The partially ice-covered water sparkled in the sun, a beguiling, shimmering place. It beckoned to me. *Beautiful... so beautiful...*

My feet found their way to the pond's edge, and I imagined Mae's laughter—her humming, "Blue like the water is the pretty dress I wear." I hummed along, drawing ever closer to the water's edge. I let my shoes sink into the cold mud, then my ankles, and then my stocking'd legs... deeper... the water reached my chin and warmth spread through my cold body. I laughed for the first time since that day.

So cold, and yet so warm... No more pain...

Mount Nebo, *at 11,928 feet, is the highest mountain in the southern-most point of the Wasatch Range and is named after the biblical Mount Nebo. Parts of the mountain are covered in snow from mid-October until July. It is a popular destination for hikers.*

13. Thistle Valley

Doug Gibson

It was a cold early September dawn in 1870. Joshua Tanner, alone, on one knee, narrowed his eyes, trying to capture a better sight of the valley. The dark was mostly gone, the ground dewy, and faint mists of fog served as a transparent curtain.

Twenty-one-year-old Josh was on Indian patrol, keeping an eye out for renegade Paiutes who had graduated from stealing cattle to burning farms and, if rumors were correct, killing isolated travelers. Behind him, 50 yards uphill, the members of his militia slept.

Josh's shift would be up when the company horn blew twice. From his post, he looked down on a meadow and a rising covered with trees. Beyond that the Thistle valley stretched out. The view allowed for proper advance notice of an Indian attack.

Josh's keen ears heard a slight rustle, and his eyes moved toward the sound. Beyond the trees a figure came into view. Josh was patient, watching as he fixed his rifle on the approaching form. It was an Indian. He carried a dead sheep over his shoulders. Josh squinted, trying to make out what the Indian was wearing. His eyes registered surprise. It was an Army uniform. *Probably belongs to someone he killed*, Josh thought.

Without hesitation, Josh fired his rifle and the Indian fell. Beyond him a dozen men awoke with alarm. "All's well, shot a Paiute," Josh yelled. Keeping his rifle out, Josh ran to the victim. He was on his back, a neat bullet hole through his uniform at the chest. He was clearly dead, and Josh relaxed.

As he stood above the corpse, a hand, which had been limp, *dead*, at the Indian's side flashed out. It was holding a knife. The corpse stabbed Josh in the lower, meaty part of his left calf. Josh screamed. The corpse grinned, laid its hand down, and was still again. Seconds later, help arrived. The dead Indian was buried in a shallow grave. Josh was treated.

Two days later, the Ghost Dance commenced. It was a sacred ceremony in which members of the tribe sought to raise the spirits of those unjustly killed by Mormons and gentiles, during this conflict. Joshua Tanner's victim heeded that call.

September 2014.

It was a warmer September dawn 144 years later. Grey-haired, stooped Cade Tanner, grandson of Joshua Tanner, walked through the high grass of Thistle Valley. Kicking the dirt softly with his boots, he walked toward the ruined home. He peered through the high window and looked at the packed earth, a permanent ground floor in the attic.

It had been 31 years since the rains, the flood, and the mudslide that had erased a tiny town called Thistle. Cade had once slept in this attic, had been one of several hundred souls who had existed in Thistle, either to support the train that snaked through the valley, or to herd sheep, as Cade himself had done.

But that was a long time ago, and Cade was 85 years old now. His sheep-herding and general labor days were long gone. He lived in a three-room, $330-dollar-a-month box in Spanish Fork. Without debts, his Social Security easily covered the bills. Cade wanted for little. Once a month he drove his rusty truck within a few miles of the old ghost town and hiked through what he still called Thistle Valley, with a rucksack over his shoulder and a rifle in his hands. At night he camped, and marveled how a mudslide had bullied a mountain into retreat, blocking a river and moving water and mud over most of a town.

It was early fall, dry but chilly. Cade walked a half hour through the valley, eyes away from the ruins, hearing sounds magnified by silence: motors from the nearby highways that had been re-routed from Thistle, the scurries of small game in the grass. But no sounds made by humans, other than Cade.

Thistle was a dead town, just as the Cade Tanner family was a dead family. There had been two mostly good years, very long ago, with his wife, Eula, but the joy had petered out of the union. Three years after their marriage, with a toddler and a baby roaming around, they had stared blankly at each other, wondering who this person was they had madly made love with over and over just two years ago. She had left with the older child, the girl Colleen, leaving Cade with the boy, Bronze, who was starting to totter around steadily at eighteen months.

Cade's father, Sam Tanner, who had also lost his wife's love, insisted it was the curse of the Ghost Dance. "Daddy Joshua killed the *injun,* who just wanted to eat, and now we're cursed forever; no Tanner man is capable of being loved!" But Cade paid no heed to tall tales, and besides, his dad died mere weeks after Eula left their home so he wasn't there to remind Cade about the curse.

With a boy at home and no one to watch him, Cade reluctantly left Thistle for Spanish Fork and the indoor drudgery of janitorial work. When the boy turned six, they began annual camping trips to Thistle Valley. They hiked through Dad's old haunts and camped in tents beneath the stars, father and son. They were the best years of Cade's life, and the memory of those yearly trips gnawed at him, hurt terribly at times, yet they were the only nourishment in his life.

Raising Bronze, so named because he was so much better than mere metal alloy, was mostly wonderful. Being his father, watching the chubby toddler turn into a boy, and eventually a strong, smart man-child, had defined parental love for Cade. The annual treks to Thistle had served as markers of the boy's growth—Bronze at six, Bronze at nine, at thirteen, seventeen . . .

Years before the flood, the year Bronze turned eight they camped at Thistle Valley as usual. It was pitch dark when Cade heard what sounded like whimpering. He reached across the small tent and gently tapped with his palm on the smaller sleeping bag to locate his son. The taps turned to desperate chops as he realized he was alone in the tent. The whimpering continued. For no reason the phrase "Ghost Dance" entered his mind.

He panicked, shimmied out of his bag, and grabbed his coat and flashlight near the tent's entrance. When he exited the tent, his hand grabbed the flap to zip it down. There was no zipper; the fabric felt harsher and thicker, with a rope hanging down on two sides. The whimpering became louder. And then he heard Bronze cry out, "No! No! Stay away, Indian!" Fear for his son dissolved his concerns over fabric and ropes.

Cade scrambled out of the tent, fumbling with what he thought was the flashlight but what instead turned out to be a rock. He dropped it outside and ran blindly toward the cries and whimpers. In full flight, he tripped on a stone and tumbled down the slope. His fall was stopped by a tree. A small hand grabbed at his ankle. "I'm scared! I'm scared!" cried Bronze. Cade's hands reached for the skinny shoulders. He traced Bronze's little-boy face with his fingers making sure he was unharmed. The boy buried his head in Cade's shoulder.

And then Cade saw the Indian. Clad in the garb of a US Cavalry officer, the Indian pointed a spear at them. Hanging over his shoulder was a freshly stripped young sheep. The Indian bared his teeth in an angry grin. He came closer.

Remembering the tales his granddad had told him, Cade closed his eyes and stammered, "You aren't real. Go away." When he opened his eyes the apparition was gone.

Cade let out a sigh of relief. He held Bronze tighter and whispered comforting words until the boy stopped trembling and began to doze. Starting to feel sleepy himself, Cade considered spending the night right where they were instead of going back to the tent—he saw the blinking lights of the town and wondered why he hadn't noticed them until the Indian had left. With an uncontrollable shudder, he now thought of the rock he had confused with his flashlight and the tent which seemed to have been more like something out of a nineteenth-century army bivouac rather than the nylon tent he knew he owned.

With his back against the tree, Cade held the sleeping boy until morning. When they both awoke, Cade could see the smoke coming out of chimneys in Thistle, and heard the train's arrival. When he went back to the tent, which once again had its flaps and zipper, he found the flashlight outside the entrance where he had tossed it, convinced it had been a rock. Now Cade didn't know what to think.

Bronze did not remember what had scared him and caused him leave their tent. But Cade knew, and decided to tell his son about Grandpa Joshua, the killing, and the ghost dance.

Bronze grew strong, with a passion for sports, girls, and, to his father's delight, a talent for building things. At eighteen, Bronze packed off to Denver, with enthusiasm, to become a carpenter's assistant, and although Cade was sorry to see him go, he felt proud of his boy.

Weeks turned into months and Cade heard nothing from his son, save occasional requests for money. And then those requests stopped. Cade went to Denver to find him, but Bronze had left.

Cade waited for news, reluctant to own the truth, even to himself. But the time came when he had to acknowledge the nagging sense that his pride in Bronze was sadly short-lived. It had to be the curse.

The call came three years after father and son had parted. It came from a sheriff in Durango. "Your son is in jail—charged with drug possession." Cade went there and found an incarcerated, too-thin Bronze, whose eyes jumped with the agony of forced withdrawal. "I'm so scared, I'm so scared . . ." the son told his father.

Cade would save his son again. He organized to have Bronze sent to a rehabilitation center in Denver, but a couple of weeks later he received a letter telling him that Bronze had run away. Another letter arrived the month Bronze would have turned 23. It came from the same Durango sheriff. Heroin overdose; Bronze was dead. Cade made another trip to Durango to collect his son's remains. He had Bronze cremated.

He immediately traveled to Thistle Valley. Its namesake town was still kicking, although the switch to diesel trains had cut the town's population to 200 or so. It was still years away from the slide.

In the pitch dark, moving south to north, Cade tossed his son's ashes into the valley. "The curse got us all, my son," the old man whispered. "The Cade Tanner family will now be a dead family."

Cade put his rifle into his mouth. But, just before he pulled the trigger, a small hand clutched his ankle. Cade dropped the rifle. He reached to his ankle. Nothing. But there was one more squeeze and then the pressure—and the spirit guiding it—was gone from Cade's senses.

Cade went home, and life passed quietly, mostly in solitude, for the next 35 years.

During that time there were three unexpected events, several years apart. Cade received an obituary notice in the mail, several months old, postmarked La Verkin, Utah. It announced Eula's death. Later came a mere death notice, two lines long, postmarked Syracuse, NY, announcing the death of Colleen Tanner. There was no mention of grandchildren. Cade was alone, and no living soul loved him. Then came the third event that devastated the old man—it involved his beloved Thistle Valley.

It was 1983 and Utah had the wettest winter on record. This was preceded by torrential summer rains. The already saturated ground could not handle the extra water with the spring melt. On April 18, Cade sat in his sparsely furnished box in Spanish Fork and read *The Salt Lake Tribune.* Seventy-two families in Thistle were evacuated "as water backed up behind millions of tons of heaving, sliding mud." The town of Thistle, where Cade grew up and where he and Bronze spent many happy hours, was now doomed. Cade's heart shuddered as he read that the town "is up to its rooftops in gray water. Thistle may be no more." The phrase "Ghost Dance" entered his mind unbidden and Cade whispered, "Will the curse ever end?"

***

And so we return to the beginning of this tale, with the 85-year-old Cade Tanner, in what remains of his beloved Thistle and its valley. He turns away from the high window of his old house—the attic which had been his room and that now is at ground level. He knows he will spend the night here, close to the valley and hills that he shared for more than a decade with his son. In Thistle Valley, the memories are bittersweet. Sitting with his back to the same tree where Cade had once saved his life, no hand squeezes his ankle because no manifestation has appeared for two generations. But this night is different. "Ghost dance" comes to Cade's mind again, and the Indian will appear.

Cade wakes up late at night. His tent is gone. He's sleeping with four rough blankets, two underneath, two above. He's wearing rough clothes. In his hand is a knife, rather than a rifle. The air smells of sheep. Cade can hear the shouts of the sheepherders. He detects panic in their voices and movements.

Without a child to worry about, Cade is cognizant of the bizarre changes. He senses a Thistle Valley of long ago. Sheepherders are running through the valley. No attention is paid to Cade. He hears voices: "Call the bishop" . . . The Indians want us out of the valley" . . . "They are everywhere." . . . "They demand sheep or they will kill" . . . "Ride for help!"

Certain he's witness to a dream, Cade moves forward through the valley. He can see their tree in the distance. Indians hold sheep that are bleating in panic. A teenage sheepherder approaches them. He is struck across the face with a rope and backs away. The other sheepherders are holding powder muskets. Some Indians have bows and arrows aimed. It's a standoff. One Indian draws a knife and slits the throat of a sheep. It is gutted rapidly. Dogs move in and, unmolested, eat the guts on the ground. The Indians, with the carcass, start to back away. The sheepherders seem satisfied to sacrifice one of their livestock to end the strife.

The scene fades away. Cade, enjoying the supernatural, walks toward the tree. It is completely dark; he sees no sheep. The dark peace is soothing. Time seems to shift. He holds a knife for a few seconds, and he holds a rifle, then a knife again. He hears the howl of a lone coyote and the hoot of an owl, which become drowned out by the sound of a distant train.

Cade is distracted by what seems to be a presence in the middle of the valley. Following his dream, Cade changes his route and approaches. The apparition is outlined in the dark. As he approaches within yards of his dream's subject, the moon allows enough light to identify the visitor. It is the Indian who had haunted Bronze. Cade can see the Cavalry officer's uniform, the buttons and medals affixed to it. The Indian is seen in profile. His eyes are directed away from Cade. They seem to be searching for something. The old man is frightened. He's about to turn away when the apparition turns its own head. It bares its teeth in the same manner it did more than a half-century ago. Its eyes, gleaming red, pierce Cade.

"This is not real," says Cade, closing his eyes, convinced he will be able to dispel the apparition like he did before. But when he opens his eyes, the evil face is mere inches from the old man. Cade whimpers. The Indian lifts Cade up and tosses him to the ground.

Jabbering in fear, Cade gets up and starts to run. The apparition grabs his shoulder and flips him around as he throws him again into the cold ground. Cade struggles up. The Indian aims the spear at him.

"No, no, stay away Indian," Cade babbles as he tries to run. A solid kick from an Army boot sends him sprawling. Unable to speak coherently now, Cade bawls and whimpers more loudly as he starts running. He runs as fast as an old man can run, but the apparition stays at his shoulder, occasionally shoving him. Cade is a mouse trapped in the vise of a crafty tom cat, to be played with until the predator is bored and ready to kill. He runs toward the tree as he did long ago and once again tumbles down the gentle hill, somersaulting until his body connects with the tree. With his back against the bark, he yells out, "I'm so scared! I'm so scared!"

The Indian approaches, but midway to its prey, it drops back. Strong arms are around Cade, comforting him. Cade, frightened to near insensibility, has his face buried in his protector's chest.

"It's okay, Dad. I'm here. You're safe," says the new apparition. It glares at the Indian ghost, daring it to move forward. The Indian puts a truculent smile on his face, remembering his own long-ago hijinks when the ghost-protector was a mortal. The specter finally shrugs its shoulders, turns, and disappears.

Father and son are alone. The son holds the father for a very long time. Cade sleeps peacefully. The curse of the Ghost dance is finally broken by the eternal bond of love between father and son.

Epilogue

Historic events and legends
of the Wasatch Mountains

Logan: In 1923, twenty miles from Logan, Frank Clark shot Old Ephraim in the head on the 22nd August with .25-35 carbine rifle. It reportedly took all seven rounds to kill the bear. Clark planned to kill the bear in 1914, but did not succeed until 1923. On the night of 21 August, he woke to "a roar and groan," and took his gun to investigate. After several unsuccessful shots, Clark finally found the bear, which had been caught in a trap that Clark had set earlier. Clark would express remorse for having to do it. Old Ephraim was skinned and buried, but was later dug up by Boy Scout Troop 43, which sent the skull to the Smithsonian where it was identified as a grizzly. At the time of his death, Old Ephraim, known as ol' three toes, stood ten feet tall and weighed 1,100 pounds.

Randolph: The town of Argyle was located about three miles southwest of Randolph, Utah. It was settled in 1875 by John Kennedy Sr. and his family. The Shoshone and Bannock Indians migrated through Rich County, often camping along Big Creek on the north end of John's property in Argyle. John was on friendly terms with these Indians and planted his garden large enough to share with them. This once busy little ranching community is now listed as a ghost town. Around 1816 or 1817, huge wolves began showing up in the valley. The settlers believed the wolves came down from Canada. These strong animals had an enormous appetite and could kill and eat an entire steer in one night. Ranchers tried trapping and hunting the wolves, but the wolves were very smart and difficult to trap. Could it be that they are still roaming the hills and mountains above Randolph and Argyle?

Brigham City: The Bushnell Military Hospital was built in Brigham City and assisted military patients (WWII), specifically amputees, from 1942 to 1946. From 1948 to 1984 it was an Indian School. During the war the grounds were meticulously kept by German POW's. In the late 1970s and early 1980s numbers of former POWs returned to show their children and grandchildren where they spent the war. Next it was used as a school. Now it houses a furniture and antique store. Until recently the school was left largely deserted. This allowed local delinquents to break windows and enter to paint graffiti. Entering these buildings is done as a sort of dare. There are several urban legends concerning the buildings. The most popular are that the buildings are haunted, or that tunnels built during WWII connecting the buildings underneath are used for satanic blood filled rituals.

Cove Point, Bear River City: The Transcontinental Railroad was completed in May of 1869, connecting the East and West of the United States by rail. Many of the laborers who worked on the project were

Chinese. The Central Pacific and the Union Pacific Railroads met at Promontory Point, Utah, near present-day Brigham City. As part of the celebration, the two sides drove a golden spike into the final rail section. Workers left the camps along the railroad grades and the Chinese abandoned their main camp at the Sinks of Dove Creek. In 1979, a ranger, Steve Ellison, experienced something that made him wonder if the workers were perhaps still there. While Ellison and a group of friends camped at Dove Creek, he took the late night guard shift along the old grade. As he patrolled the area, he heard the sound of an locomotive off in the darkness. He saw a small light coming toward him, and tiny sparks flew up from the steel rails. He also heard footsteps and what seemed like people speaking Chinese. Then it all vanished. Others saw ghost locomotives speed across the desert and pass right through solid trains. The sinks of Dove Creek are near Kelton and can be reached by a primitive railroad grade.

Huntsville is a sleepy mountain village nestled at the edge of Pineview Reservoir in Ogden Valley. At the far west edge of town, jutting out into the lake is the local cemetery, surrounded by picnic areas and beaches. Locals report sightings of a ghostly figure frequenting Cemetery Point and the road leading to it. The apparition is a small woman, draped in or dragging a shawl. Some speculate she may be the spirit of a young lady who committed suicide by walking into the lake with a backpack full of rocks.

It was said at the time of her passing she was despondent over the break-up of her family.

Ogden: Peery's Egyptian Theater is a historic Ogden movie theater on Washington Ave between 24th and 25th Street. It was built in 1923. During construction, a 12-year-old girl named Alison brought her father lunch. At some point during her visit she died in a fall, either from scaffolding that she was climbing on, or from falling from a window onto the stage. These days, the friendly ghost of Alison reportedly hangs out haunting the boxes in the rear of the theater, though there have been sightings of her playing a piano, turning lights on and off, and occasionally sitting next to a lucky patron in the audience.

Roy: After years of stories from renters, the owner of an apartment building somewhere in Roy, Utah, conceded that a young ghost girl playfully haunted his complex. Tenants in the apartment saw the girl walk past doors, look out of windows, and walk around the building. Though no other ghosts were ever seen, renters speculated the girl played with ghost _friends_, as multiple footsteps were often heard in her apartment. When the girl's residence was renovated, she was never heard or seen in the building again. Her identity is still a mystery.

Echo City, at the mouth of Echo Canyon, Summit County, UT, was settled in 1854 by James Bromley, who ran the Weber Stage Station, a stop on the

Overland Stage Route and Pony Express. The railroad soon followed, and tents, saloons, and brothels sprang up overnight. When the railroad men moved on, Echo became a ghost town. Buildings were torn down, and seven human skeletons were discovered under one saloon. Also discovered in the wall of the building was a love letter to a Pony Express rider, a five-dollar gold piece, and a pair of gold rimmed spectacles.

Park City: During the years when silver mines still operated, there were several mining accidents. In 1902 poison gas caused an explosion in the mines and many miners died. Afterward miners said they saw those who were killed haunting the tunnels, looking for their missing body parts which they lost during the explosions. There were also sightings of a harbinger dressed in a yellow slicker just before mining accidents. Others said the lower rungs of ladders mysteriously disappeared, preventing miners escaping tunnels in emergencies. Another ghost appearance was a woman with long blond hair riding a horse. She was seen as the bearer of good news.

Fort Douglas, Salt Lake City: Numerous stories are told by staff and guests of "Clem." He is described as a stocky man with dark hair and a beard, dressed in a Civil War Federal uniform. Every year, during October, the museum hosts an event in Clem's honor, telling stories of him.

Legend of Timpanogos: A Young Native American maiden, Utahna, became the one to be a sacrificed to bring rain to her tribe. While she made the climb to jump off the mountain, Red Eagle saw her and became infatuated with her beauty. He convinced her he was the god Timpanogos and told her that being his wife would complete the sacrifice. They lived in Timpanogos Cave until Utahna realized Red Eagle had tricked her. She fulfilled her duty and a broken-hearted Red Eagle found Utahna's body at the foot of the mountain and carried her back to the cave, where he died next to her. The god Timpanogos felt sorry for the loss of their perfect love and created the great heart, which are still in the cave, above the place where they died.

Heber City: A lady dressed in blue has been wandering the streets of Provo, carrying a doll also dressed in blue. When her husband went off to war their daughter died in the Provo River. The woman was afraid to tell him of their child's death on his return. So, she dressed a doll to look like the girl so her husband wouldn't be mad. When her husband died, she didn't believe it and she can still be found, carrying the doll, walking the streets of the Timberlake's, waiting for his return.

Thistle Valley: The Native American "ghost dance" is a long-established ritual. It originated among the Paiutes of Nevada. It's a sacred ceremony in which living members of the tribe seek the return of those who have died at the hands of persecutors. Massacres, including Wounded Knee, derived in part from Caucasians terrified that the ghost dance was a call to end white domination. A generation earlier, however, in Utah, during and after The Black Hawk War, ghost dances were often invoked in valleys and plains by natives who wished to bring back their own who's been slain by the Mormons and other white settlers. Thistle Valley wasn't immune to these conflicts, and the supernatural occurred there, too. The ghost dances were indeed successful at raising the spirits of the aggrieved dead. Once a spirit is summoned, repeat visits are expected. Even today, if one traverses the lonely, deserted valley near Thistle, the shouts, oaths, and screams of conflict—and encounters with those who want retribution—are not dreams.

Acknowledgements

My sincere thanks goes to the talented authors in this book. It would not have been possible if not for you—Barbara, Brenda, Christy, Dimitria, Doug, Jodi, Lynda, Michele, Sherry, and Vicki. Your creative writing and research shines through the telling of your tales. You **are** storytellers!

For two of these authors, the journey started at the beginning, with *Tales from Huntsville, Eden, Liberty and Beyond (Out of print).* Lynda Scott and Dimitria Van Leeuwen had stories in that anthology and every subsequent book in the TALES series, right along with me. Lynda and Dimitria—it's been a pleasure!

After reading the book, residents of the towns featured in this publication, might look differently at their surroundings—especially on dark and stormy nights.

My everlasting love and gratitude goes to Johan, who is, and always has been, supportive in all of my endeavors even if they don't make any sense *at all*.

Blessings to the *Writing Divas*—Christy, Michele, Patricia, Jodi, Sherry, and Dimitria. Thank you for your loving support and help. Kudos to Janet Battisti, Vince Font, Marcia Lusk, Wendy Toliver, and Stan Trollip, who took time from their busy lives to review this book. Love always to Wendy, whose encouragement makes me believe that dreams do come true.

Last but not least, cheers to Zoë Sharp for writing the introduction to this book. You are truly an inspiration.

To our readers: Thank you for buying this book. I now dare you to choose a rainy, cold autumn day, curl up on a comfy chair in front of a fireplace, and read these tales from the dark and stormy minds of these talented authors.

Drienie Hattingh

*My special thanks to Barbara Emanuelson who stepped up to the plate and accepted the challenge of writing a new story, within **one** week, for this revised version of Tales From the Wasatch to replace a story in this book. Your story made this book so much more special, Barbara! Thank you!*

About the Authors

Drienie Hattingh has been a columnist for eighteen years. Her articles appeared in newspapers and magazines in America and South Africa. Her essays have been published in *Christmas Miracles, The Spirit of Christmas and a Hallmark gift book, Lessons from My Parents and Chicken Soup for the Soul.* Her novella, *A Glass Slipper for Christmas,* was published in 2013 and a short horror story, *The Last Gas Station* in 2014. She is the publisher of the TALES SERIES and has 8 stories in these anthologies. She loves to knit and spend time with her family, especially her grandsons, Simon and Tristan. Drienie and her husband, Johan, live on Historic 25th Street in Ogden, Utah. She's a member of LUW and the Writing Divas.

DrienieM@aol.com

Jodi Orgill Brown grew up in Virginia, but has spent twenty years living all over the Wasatch Front. Jodi earned degrees from BYU and the University of Utah. She is a Writing Diva and an award-winning member of the League of Utah Writers. Jodi and Tolan Brown have four children.

lifeconstructionzone@gmail.com

Vicki Droogsma was born in England and raised in California. She now lives in Ogden, Utah, with her wonderful supportive family. Her first published story, "The Dare," found in *Tales from Two-Bit Street and Beyond... Part II*, is her proudest accomplishment. Vicki loves writing and hopes to continue to create more tales in the future.

Viledra@yahoo.com

Barbara Emanualson is an award-winning author and educator. She is the author of the historical romance *Through Tempest Forged* (Community Press, 2007). As a champion for literacy, she has many works in process, including historical fiction for adults and children. A former resident of Pleasant View, Utah, she now resides in Wilmington, North Carolina.

bpemanuelson@gmail.com

Doug Gibson lives in Ogden with his wife, Kati, and three children. He's the Opinion Editor at the *Standard-Examiner* daily newspaper. A native of Long Beach, California, he has also lived in Boston, Massachusetts, and Ely, Nevada. He served an LDS mission long ago in Peru.

His passion is reading.

doug1963@gmail.com

Brenda Hattingh lives in Salt Lake City, Utah, with her doggy, Wyatt. She's the owner of a children's entertainment company *Boobiliboo!* She's also a songwriter and has a band, *SugarTown Alley*, in which she is one of the lead singers and plays the guitar. Another one of Brenda's jobs is being an art instructor at the *Paintmixer.* In her spare time she does pet portraits and is also a magician's assistant. She loves to travel.

Boobiliboo@gmail.com

Sherry Hogg writes for fun and self-fulfillment. Her picture book, *Child of Mine*, a mommy love story, is loved by mommies and children of all ages. Sherry enjoyed raising her four kids in the beautiful Ogden Valley, but now resides in Pleasant View with her boyfriend and three basset hounds.

justmybooks@hotmail.com

Michele McKinnon got her Master's degree in Accounting from Weber State University. She's an avid reader and turned her love of the written word into her own writing. Her stories were published in *Tales from Two-Bit Street and Beyond, Part I and II.* She loves gardening and playing with her grandkids. She lives in Bountiful, Utah, and is a member of the League of Utah Writers and The Writing Divas.

michele_mckinnon@yahoo.com

Christy Monson retired as a Licensed Marriage and Family Therapist. She's an award-winning author of: *Texting Through Time*, a children's book series; *Becoming Free... A Woman's Guide to Internal Strength*, a self-help book; and *Love, Hugs, and Hope*, a children's self-help book.

Her articles have been published in Familius, Gospel Ideals, and Modern Molly Mormon.

http://christymonson.blogspot.com/
http://www.christymonson.com/index.html

Lynda West Scott worked as a private investigator for 25 years. Since then she has written magazine articles and worked as a copy editor. One of her essays appears in *Lessons From My Parents* and she has stories in all of the Tales series. She and her husband, Mike, recently moved from Utah to California, to be closer to their grandchildren.

lynda_scott@msn.com

Dimtiria Van Leeuwen has a varied background, including experience as a belly-dance teacher, photographer, singing telegram messenger, mixed-media artist and musician. She is one of the lead singers in the Utah band, *SugarTown Alley*. Her stories, *Jelly, Kitten, Gibson Girl and Recipe for Reclamation*, are published in the Tales series.

dimitria.vl@gmail.com

Authors of Tales from the Wasatch at Ogden Union Station.

Made in the USA
Columbia, SC
12 January 2022

53605619R00111